Stalking
Shadows

S.A. Hunter

The Scary Mary Series
Scary Mary
Stalking Shadows
Broken Spirits (coming August 2013)

Other books by S.A. Hunter
Unicorn Bait
Dragon Prey (coming October 2013)

Cover design by S.A. Hunter

Smoke image courtesy of Suwit Ritjaroon
from FreeDigitalPhotos.net

ISBN-13: 978-1490457345

ISBN-10: 1490457348

DEDICATION

As always, thank you to my parents for their love and support, a special thank you to Rya for her excellent help in editing this story (though any mistakes are still all my fault), and thank you to all the fans who have given me encouragement and help along the way.

CONTENTS

CHAPTER 1

Boy Troubles

Mary looked around the dimly lit, white room in confusion. She didn't know where she was or how she'd gotten there. The last thing she remembered was going to sleep in her bedroom. Everything had a weird fuzzy quality about it. She rubbed her eyes to clear her vision, but the fuzziness didn't go away.

"Mary, I need your help," said someone from behind her. She turned, and her stomach dropped. She'd been alone in the small, white room, but now, Vicky Nelson sat propped up in a hospital bed with a gauze bandage circling her head.

"What's going on?" Mary asked.

"Geez, you're slow. We're dreaming."

"What?"

Vicky rolled her eyes. "Pinch yourself."

Mary stared at the other girl for a second and then pinched herself carefully on the arm.

She didn't feel it. "I'm dreaming?"

"No, we're dreaming."

"No, you mean me. I'm dreaming, and you're the monster in my nightmare."

Vicky crossed her arms and stared down her nose at Mary. "I can't believe you're the only person who can help me."

Mary mirrored her by crossing her arms as well. "And why would I ever want to help you?" Vicky Nelson had been her arch nemesis since third grade when the auburn-haired girl had christened her with her nickname Scary Mary. Since then, Vicky had taunted Mary, ridiculed her, and spread lies about her. Mary loathed her with every fiber of her being.

Vicky didn't have an answer.

Mary looked Vicky over more closely. The bandage circled her head holding in place a lump of gauze on the left side of her forehead. She had an IV connected to her arm and various monitors connected to her body. She could trace the lines back to their respective machines. She didn't know what some of the machines did, but they beeped and blinked quietly on their own.

"Well, you're not getting a kidney," Mary said.

"Like I'd want one of your mutant organs. That's not the type of help I need."

Of course, Vicky was still Vicky even in a

dream. Mary turned her back to the other girl and began looking for an exit.

"Hey, come back here!"

"No," she replied. She still didn't see a door, but there had to be a way out. She'd settle for a window or an air vent. "Where's the exit?"

"You're not going anywhere. Not until you listen to me."

Maybe she could teleport out like on Star Trek? She closed her eyes and thought really hard about leaving. She cracked open one eye, but no joy. She was still in a little white room with a very awful person.

"Will you pay ATTENTION?"

"No, I won't pay attention, but I will pay to leave." Why wasn't the dream going her way? What sort of messed up dream was this? She didn't have any control. Maybe she wasn't dreaming. Maybe she'd been abducted by aliens, and Vicky was their Pod Queen!

"God, you are so weird," the other girl muttered.

Still ignoring Vicky, Mary went to the wall and began running her hands over it in an attempt to find a hidden door. If she wasn't dreaming, how had she gotten there? She wasn't finding a hidden door. She stepped back and looked around the room again. If she wasn't dreaming and this wasn't a spaceship, then the only other possibility was that she'd died and gone to hell, but had she really been so bad as to get stuck with Vicky for eternity?

"Oh, like being stuck with you would be heavenly."

She turned to the hospital bed in surprise. She knew she hadn't said that out loud. Being stuck with a mind-reading Vicky had to be another level deeper in hell.

Vicky glowered at her. She clearly had heard that thought too. "What am I doing here?" Mary asked aloud.

"If you'd pay attention, I'd tell you."

Mary waited for her to continue. Vicky sat in the hospital bed with her arms still crossed and a scowl on her face. Except for the bandage around her head, she looked normal. Maybe the cheerleader was in for a psych consult?

"Oh, ha ha. Very funny."

"What am I doing here, Vicky?" Mary asked again.

Vicky's eyes slanted away from her, and she hunched her shoulders. "I don't know how to explain it. I don't know any of that hocus-pocus lingo."

"Hocus-pocus lingo?" She was getting exasperated.

"Okay, here's the deal, I'm in a coma, and I need your help because there's something here that's trying to get me. I don't know what it is, but it's spooky weird, and you're the queen of spooky weird, so you're the only one who can help me."

"Spooky weird?" She was getting tired of Vicky's vocabulary, or rather, her "hocus-pocus lingo".

"Yeah. So bring a Ouija board or something and get rid of it!"

"Whatever. Look up 'coma' in the diction-ary. Being awake and talkative is not comatose."

"Get a clue! We're both unconscious. Like I said, we're sharing a dream."

No, this was definitely a nightmare. Help Vicky? What the hell? She went over to the wall and began kicking it. She was busting out. No more waiting for Scotty to beam her up, no more waiting for little green men, no more stewing in hell, no more talking to Vicky.

"What are you doing?"

"Leaving. Please don't follow me."

Vicky thrashed about in her bed. It made her look like a landed fish. "I don't like this any more than you do, but who else can help me?"

She kept kicking at the wall. Nothing was happening. Her shoes weren't even scuffing it. She stopped in frustration.

She turned back to Vicky. She was the key to this somehow. "What do you mean we're sharing a dream?"

"Um, just what I said. Haven't you done this before?"

"No."

"Yeah, right. Anyway, you're here, I'm here. You might as well listen to me."

Through gritted teeth, she asked, "Can you describe the spooky weirdness?" Maybe if she let her subconscious get whatever this was over with, then she'd get back to her regularly scheduled dream of purple walruses lip-synching Queen songs. The way their whiskers jumped up and down was hypnotic.

"I don't know. I'm in a coma, remember? I just feel this chill, and it's like something is pulling on me. I know whatever it is isn't right. It's evil."

"And you want me to get rid of it?"

"You or Buffy the Vampire Slayer, if you have her number. Ooh, is Buffy real? Or maybe Angel? I'd much rather have a big, handsome vampire working on this."

Mary started looking for something to kill Vicky with. That would be one sure way to end this. There was nothing obvious. She closed her eyes and imagined a guillotine with all of her willpower. A nice, big guillotine. When she opened her eyes, there was no guillotine, but Vicky was staring at her with disdain. "You're the one who needs a psych consult."

She clenched her jaw to keep from screaming. Being stuck in a room with her least favorite person without any way to escape was maddening. She'd played nice. She'd let Vicky tell her about the spooky weirdness. Where was the door?

"Mary, open your eyes." She looked over at Vicky in confusion. She wasn't the one who'd spoken.

"Open your eyes, Mary. Time to wake up."

She blinked. The room warped and wavered.

"You better come by the hospital!" Vicky shouted through the distortion.

"Wake up, Mary. Open your eyes. I made French toast."

She opened her eyes and looked at Gran in relief. "Thank God! I thought that dream would never end."

Gran grinned as she folded back her blankets. "What was the dream about?"

"This girl from school, who I hate. She was insisting I had to help her with something. It was awful. I was trapped."

"Well, it's morning now. Get dressed and let's go have something to eat."

She eagerly slid out of bed. She'd have to have a long talk with herself before she fell asleep again. Nightmares of Vicky were just un-called-for. She saw enough of the vapid cheer-leader when she was awake.

~ ~ ~

Mary closed her locker slowly as she debat-ed whether to fake sick to go home or suffer out the rest of the day. It was only TAB, the fifteen-minute break between first and second period. She usually didn't start thinking about faking nausea until third period. It was going to be a long day.

She turned to head to class and walked straight into someone. "Sheesh, could you move?" she said.

"Hey, Mary, how are you doing?" She forgot her annoyance when she saw who she'd walked into. Kyle wasn't exactly a friend, but she didn't dislike him either. He had a bit of a hero-worship thing for her, which, well, she really liked and couldn't bring herself to squelch. The fact that a guy on the wrestling team looked up to her really helped her ego.

"I'm fine." She was a little flummoxed by Kyle's sudden interest in her well-being. Sure, the big lug looked up to her, but he usually kept away from her. She made the other wrestlers nervous.

He blinked and looked at her a bit longer. "What?"

"You haven't heard?"

"Heard what?"

He slouched and rubbed a hand over his buzz-cut head. When his mouth twisted into a grimace, she felt her own mouth mirror the twist. She braced herself for the bad news. Had Rachel gotten expelled? Was the school switching to uniforms? Compulsory pep rallies? What?

"Cy and Vicky were in a car accident."

The news hit her like a bucket of ice water. She quickly told herself not to freak out. If it had been really bad, she would've heard about it before now. It would've been on the news or something. Kyle wouldn't have been her first source of information.

"Is he okay?"

Kyle gave her a small rueful grin at the exclusion of Vicky in her question. He knew how Mary felt about her. The whole school district knew how she felt about Vicky "The Hickey" Nelson. Her nightmare flittered up in her mind. Weird. She'd dreamed about Vicky in the hospital, and now she'd been in an accident. Had the dream been precognitive? But why would she suddenly get a glimpse of Vicky's future?

"Cy broke a collar bone and dislocated his shoulder, but he'll be all right. He was discharged from the hospital yesterday."

"Yesterday? When was the accident?"

"Saturday night."

"Huh." She tried not to feel disappointment at being left out of the loop for so long. Cy wasn't her boyfriend, but she couldn't believe he hadn't called her. She'd thought they were friends, with the possibility of more in the future.

"I can't believe he didn't call you."

Having Kyle echo her thoughts snapped her out of her gloom. "You said he's fine, right? He probably thought it was no big deal."

"His arm's in a sling, and he's got broken bones."

"Bones mend. Slings are removable," she said, not meeting his eyes. She really wanted him to shut up and go away.

"Vicky's in a coma."

That jerked her head up. "What?"

"She's been a coma since the accident. She's not on life support, but she can't wake up. I heard she may not wake up for a while."

"For real?" Goose bumps formed on her arms. Her dream was coming true. She mulled that over. Before this news, the fantasy of Vicky being in a coma would've made her smile whimsically. The reality of Vicky in a coma didn't give her any sense of whimsy.

"Yeah, Cy's been sitting with her. He feels responsible. He was the one driving, but it wasn't his fault. Another car hydroplaned across the road and hit them head-on. They were both wearing their seat belts, but the SUV rolled, and well, they both got hurt pretty bad. The SUV's totaled."

"God, that's awful." She hoped the SUV hadn't landed on its roof. Her family's sedan had. She'd been so confused. Mom had told her everything would be okay and not to be scared. Only problem was, Mom's lips hadn't moved. "Were the people in the other car hurt?"

Kyle shook his head. "Not bad, they only had bumps and bruises. The police are going to charge them with reckless driving or some-thing."

She looked at the hallway floor. This was a lot to process. "Mary, there's something else--"

"They were on a date," she said. She glanced up for confirmation. His face was pinched, but he nodded. She'd known Vicky was interested in Cy and that they'd been hanging out some. She hadn't known it had progressed this far.

"Thanks for telling me, Kyle."

He gave her a nod and touched her arm. "If you need updates, just ask."

She gave him a tiny smile. "Thanks."

The bell for class sounded. She needed to

head to second period. She didn't feel well. It was like there was a pit in her stomach. Not a gaping hole pit, but like a fruit pit. It was round, hard, and had a sharp point that poked at her. She wanted to throw it up. She didn't need to fake nausea now. She really felt sick.

She and Cy had gone on one date that had ended with Vicky crashing it, him yelling at Mary, and the whole school whispering that Mary was some kind of witch. Things had died down. It had become old news, but she and Cy hadn't hung out outside of school since then. He'd eaten lunch with her a couple of times, and they still sat together in English, but that was it. She knew Vicky had been pursuing him. She'd made her interest in him well known, but Mary hadn't thought he would really take the cheerleader seriously. They'd bonded over trashtalking Vicky in the first place. It made her angry that he'd finally bent to the popular girl's will.

He'd been the only boy in school who'd ever shown any interest in Mary, and she'd liked him. Now he was hanging out at the hospital bedside of another girl, a girl who was popular, pretty, and absolutely normal. The pit poked her.

~ ~ ~

She went outside to have lunch with Rachel in their usual spot. She sat down in the grass and waited. The sun felt nice and warmed her back, though there was a hint of autumn chill in the air. Other students were scattered about, sitting in clumps as well. Her best friend joined her a few minutes later.

"How you doin'?" Rachel asked.

She gave her best friend the biggest, fakest smile she could muster.

"Geez, that bad?"

She turned away and shrugged. News certainly traveled fast. She'd caught a few people whispering and pointing at her in the halls. They were probably debating how she'd caused the accident. Maybe she'd sacrificed a black cat or made a voodoo doll. The rumors didn't bother her. What bothered her was the fact that Cy had gone on a date with Vicky and hadn't told her. What was that about? Had he kept it a secret because he'd known it would upset her? Or had he just not thought to tell her because she wasn't important enough to tell? Maybe they weren't actually friends. She'd thought they were still that, at least. But obviously, she was behind the times. Maybe she should start reading the school newspaper. It had probably been on the front page: Queen Bee Gets Her Prince! Stupid Scary Mary Clueless! Well, she thought the school paper was stupid. Their comic strips sucked.

Mary dug out her lunch bag. In a flat voice, she said, "Vicky's in a coma. Yay."

"How'd you hear?"

"Kyle told me. What have you heard?"

"That Cy was driving Vicky home from a movie when a car crashed into them. Their car rolled, and Cy got a broken collar bone and a dislocated shoulder, and Vicky's in a coma."

"I wonder what movie they went to see." Mary didn't know if her interest was ghoulish or pathetic. She bit her tongue to keep herself from wondering aloud if they'd gotten two popcorns or one to share. That would be pathetic to ask. She'd shared popcorn with Cy when she'd been at his house.

"That's not important."

She looked at Rachel. She must not have looked good because Rachel rolled her head back and growled in frustration. "You cannot let this bother you. It was one stupid date."

"One stupid date that I know of. Have they been dating? Did you know they were going out?"

"Yes, of course I knew because I've been secretly stalking Vicky all this time. I have a small shrine to her in my closet. Every night, I burn bubblegum incense and cuddle a Kleenex she once sneezed into while I Photoshop her picture onto the covers of Glamour and Vogue."

Mary slumped and picked at her sandwich, tearing off small pieces of crust and throwing them into the grass. "So, you don't know if this was their first date or their fifth?"

"If they were a couple, Vicky would've had T-shirts made. It was probably their first date, and she tricked him into going. He probably thought he was taking her grandpa to the airport or something, and she gave him directions to the movie theater instead, and since she already had pre-purchased tickets, why not go see the movie because both of Vicky's grandfathers are dead."

"Nah, she probably shot him with a tranquilizer gun and drove him to the movie theater, and he came to as the credits rolled."

"Even more likely. So see, not as bad as you think."

"I don't know. He's obviously worried about her, which means he cares, which means he likes her, which means they're totally a couple. Right this moment, he's probably hanging out by her bedside like Prince Charming hovering over Sleeping Beauty, and I'm the evil witch trying to train some flying monkeys to whisk him away."

"Wasn't the Sleeping Beauty villainess named Maleficent? And she didn't have flying monkeys. That was the Wicked Witch of the West."

"I'm sure the Wicked Witch of the West would've loaned her some flying monkeys. They were probably pals, trading potions and stuff."

"So I'm the Wicked Witch of the West?"

"No, I always imagined you more as a Mad Madam Mim."

Rachel stared at her for a few blinks. "You've thought about this?"

"The villains are more interesting."

"Let's focus on something else."

"What?"

"Well, I'm gonna flunk biology and be disowned by my father."

"I told you taking that AP class was going to be tough. You should've stuck with CP like me."

Rachel fell back onto the grass. "I know, but Dad was going on and on about how I have to take some advanced placement courses, and I wasn't about to try AP History or AP English."

"And you wanted to dissect stuff."

"Dissecting stuff is cool. I need to take these classes if I'm going to be a coroner."

Mary shivered. Rachel had recently decided her life's goal was to be a coroner, and it freaked Mary out. She dealt with ghosts, so she knew a good bit about death, but she didn't want to know the science of it. She didn't want to face the physical evidence. The spiritual evidence was enough for her.

"If you need help studying, I can quiz you. I may only be in lowly college prep, but I do know how to read."

Rachel lifted her head and grinned. "Thanks. Maybe we could get together Wednesday. I have a test on Thursday, and I have to ace it to start getting my grade up."

Mary nodded. Helping Rachel would keep her from obsessing over Cy.

"So Kyle told you about Cy and Vicky?"

She was surprised that Rachel was going back to that topic. "Yeah, he found me during TAB. He was upset, as well that Cy hadn't told me about the accident."

"That was nice of him."

"Yeah, it was better hearing it from him than overhearing it in the hallway or something."

"He's been pretty nice to you since Ricky." Ricky was the nasty ghost that had possessed Kyle and made him try to kill her. After all that, she'd figured he'd avoid her like the plague or maybe pick on her more, but instead, he said hi to her in the hallways and openly talked to her. It surprised her because she could count on one hand the number of people who were nice to her.

"Yeah, he's still grateful that I helped him. I figure it'll die down in a while."

"I don't know. He doesn't seem so much

grateful as interested in you."

Mary looked at her in confusion. "He's just being nice. Sure, he was a complete meathead to me when I first met him, but he's mellowed since then."

Rachel didn't reply. Mary shrugged it off and finished eating her lunch.

"Wasn't Mad Madam Mim like kind of dumpy and crazy?"

"She could make herself look however she wanted. She chose to look dumpy, but she was definitely crazy."

"Huh."

"It's how I picture you at seventy."

"You know, I sometimes can't wait to be old. Old people get away with the best stuff."

"I know, just look at Gran."

~ ~ ~

Mary worked on her homework in the living room. She was also tossing a red squeaky ball across the room. It would float back to her, and she'd toss it again. It was either toss the ball or have Chowder, their little ghost dog, whining at her feet. His body currently sat on top of the television. It was his anchor. Ghosts needed physical objects to tie them to the earth. Anchors could be anything. Ricky's had been a locket.

Becca, a little girl ghost who'd terrorized Mary when she was six, had anchored to a doll. But Chowder's anchor couldn't have been more obvious. He was a ghost, but he still had his body. He just couldn't move it, which was good. Having a zombie dog would be even worse than a phantom one.

Gran was finishing up with a new client. Mary had placed an order for a large pizza to be delivered. It should arrive any minute. She was still bummed about the Vicky/Cy thing, but it was slowly sinking away.

She heard a car start up behind the house, and a few moments later, Gran came through the beaded curtains. Mary closed her textbook and put down her pencil. "How'd the session go?"

Gran smoothed back her grey hair and took a seat. "Mrs. Beadley is having some trouble with her dead husband."

"What sort of trouble?"

"Dating mainly. He doesn't like the fact that his widow is getting back into the game. If she brings a man over, he makes the lights flicker or the radio come on to frighten away her date. She's at her wit's end." The red ball dropped at Gran's feet. She tossed it across the room.

"He hasn't tried to hurt her, has he?"

"Oh no, nothing like that. She seems positive

he'd never escalate that far. She remembers him quite fondly, but he's annoying her a great deal now. She thinks it's time for him to move on, like she's trying to do." The ball floated back to her, and she picked it up again.

"Any ideas about how to deal with him?"

"I think I'll have to go to their home. She doesn't have any idea what he could be anchored to."

"Do you want me to go with you?"

Gran sighed and looked down at the squeaky ball in her hands. "I shouldn't ask, but I think your presence could help."

"It's no problem. If he's as harmless as you say, it'll be fine."

The doorbell rang, and Gran got up to get the pizza. She tossed the squeaky ball to Mary. Chowder barked.

Mary pretended not to hear him while the door was open. Once the door was closed, she threw the ball as far as she could to get rid of Chowder for a bit.

"Did anything happen at school today?" Gran asked as she gave her a pizza slice on a paper plate.

She eagerly took a bite of her pizza, nodding her head while she chewed. "Cy and Vicky Nelson were in a car accident over the weekend. Cy broke his collarbone and dislocated a shoulder.

wouldn't enjoy dark, cold, Arctic plateaus. Mary sat back and got colder. Most people preferred sunny, warm, tropical islands. That's why they were popular destinations. Dark, cold, Arctic plateaus didn't get many tourists. And the few who did go had probably meant to take the plane to Cozumel. Maybe Cy had gotten on the wrong plane. He'd tried to play it off as intentional, but he'd sneaked off to warmer climes when he'd gotten the chance.

When the bell rang, she gathered her things. "I'll go make copies of my notes in the library. Do you want to wait at the front of school for me to bring them out?"

He hung his book bag on his good shoulder. "No, I'll go with you."

She didn't reply and exited the room. They walked in silence to the library while students streamed around them in the opposite direction. She caught herself glancing back to make sure Cy wasn't getting jostled by the other students. Walking against the flow in a crowd had to be dangerous for his arm. She felt like a chump for worrying about him.

She entered the library and went to the copier. Another student was already using it. She stood back to wait. Cy came up beside her. He held out his hand. It had a dollar in change in it.

"Here."

She took the change stiffly and set about ignoring him again. It was what one was supposed to do with strangers.

"I knew you'd be upset if you heard I went out with her."

She stopped ignoring him. "Oh, so now we can talk about it?"

He winced. "I didn't want to try explaining it in notes with my right hand."

"Was it your first date?"

"Officially, yeah."

"There were unofficial dates?"

"We'd gotten together a few times to study, and there were group things."

"You hung out with her friends?"

His back stiffened. "It was Key Club stuff. She'd joined, too."

"So you hung out in Key Club and studied together. For someone who doesn't like her, you sure do hang out with her a lot."

"I don't dislike her."

She had figured that out, but hearing Cy say it still felt like a punch in the gut. "Hanging out with me must really piss her off."

"She's not thrilled about it, but she can't pick my friends. She knows that, and she's cool with it, but I guess my friends think they can pick who I date."

Mary's eyes widened. She couldn't believe

he'd said that. "Oh no, you don't get to play it like that. I was never the bad guy here. You didn't tell me squat. I didn't even know you liked her. In fact, I thought you didn't like her, Mr. 'I could feel my IQ dropping from osmosis,' now suddenly, you two are dating? What? When? How?"

"You forgot where."

"I know where. The movie theater. What did you two see?"

"Moon Rain."

She was really starting to hate this conversation. She, Rachel, and Cy had talked about going to see that movie together. It would've been their first non-school outing together since the séance. She looked over at the copier and hurried to it when she saw it was free. She needed to get away from him. Forget dreams with a non-comatose Vicky, this was a nightmare.

She slapped her notebook onto the scanner bed and fed the quarters into the machine. She hit the green button.

"Look, I'm sorry I kept my thing with Vicky from you, but I didn't want to make it into a big drama, especially if nothing happened. It was one date. We aren't a couple."

"Now she's in a coma, and you're sitting by her bedside until she wakes up." She flipped a page and jabbed the green copy button.

"I'm worried about her."

"Is it just worry? Would you have gone out with her again if the accident hadn't happened?"

He didn't reply. She halfway ripped out a page of her notes as she turned it to scan the final sheet. When the last page spat out, she grabbed up the sheets, shoved them at him, and stormed out of the library.

"Mary!"

She ignored him. It was what one was supposed to do with strangers.

She walked down the hall toward the stairs. She was trying hard not to think, because she didn't like anything currently swirling around in her head. She needed a distraction, something to take her mind off Cy, Vicky, and the joke that was her love life. She couldn't stop the gurgling laugh that came out at the thought of her having a love life. Who was she kidding?

"Mary?"

She tried to pretend to not hear Kyle, but he didn't get the hint that she didn't want to talk. "Hey, Mary, wait up."

She stopped and turned toward him, but she couldn't bring herself to raise her eyes from the floor. "If you're looking for Cy, he's in the library."

"Thanks, but he'll find me. I'm not his nursemaid."

She smiled thinly and turned towards the stairs.

"Are you all right?"

She didn't turn around. "I'm peachy. See ya, Kyle." She began walking to the stairs.

"Mary, wait!" She didn't stop. Instead, she picked up her pace. She needed to get away from school. It was way past time for this day to be over. She couldn't take anymore.

She was halfway down the stairs when Kyle called down to her from the top. "He's a jerk. You shouldn't let him bother you."

She stopped and looked up at him. "That's rich, coming from you."

His face fell. She knew it was wrong to have said that, but she was hurting and wanted to lash out. Kyle wasn't one of the people hurting her, but one of those people was in a coma, and the other had an arm in a sling. She couldn't lash out at them. She shook her head.

"Don't listen to me, Kyle. I'm a jerk, too." She turned and finished going down the stairs. He didn't call out to her again.

As she was walking home, Rachel rolled up in her mom's station wagon. "Get in. We have some serious cramming to do."

The whole drama with Cy had made her totally forget her promise to help Rachel study. She climbed into the car. "Sorry, I got held up after class."

Rachel looked her over. Mary knew she didn't look good. "You still up for this?" she asked. Mary nodded. Rachel began driving again. They were headed to the library. "Did you talk to Cy today?"

She sighed and slumped down. "Yeah."

"And?"

"He likes Vicky. He knew it would upset me if he told me. They're totally a couple."

"Seriously?"

She nodded again. Rachel shook her head in silent commiseration. Mary straightened in her car seat. "I'm done dwelling on it. Let's get you all biology-ed up."

"Now you're talking."

"Hey, did your crafts teacher agree to write the recommendation?"

"Yeah, but Dad said that if I don't get my grade up in biology, he won't let me volunteer. I have to ace this test."

"Wow, that's like even more incentive to study hard."

"You say incentive. I say pressure."

"You're gonna ace it. Where are the flash cards?" She reached into the back and grabbed Rachel's book bag.

Rachel's eyebrows rose. "I think studying in the car on the way to the library is like an example of the absolute opposite of procrastination. Is there even a word for that?"

"We're studying bio, not English. Now, while studying a cell through an electron microscope, you note the following: numerous ribosomes, a well-developed endoplasmic reticulum, chloroplasts, and a cell wall. What did this cell come from?"

"A plant."

She flipped the card. "Correct!" She flipped to the next card. "The bonding of two amino acid molecules to form a larger molecule requires what?"

"The release of a water molecule."

She flipped the card. "Correct again!"

"You know Mr. Hutchins said that you shouldn't allow too many distractions while driving, or you could end up in an accident."

Mary looked through the windshield. "We're at a stoplight."

"One should always be vigilant."

She tucked the cards back into Rachel's book bag. "Fine, but we're getting through all of them at the library."

"But don't you want to do some research into Vicky's demonic stalker?"

"And how am I supposed to search for it? I don't know anything about it except it claws at her."

"Vicky didn't tell you anything else?"

"No, she didn't." And put a definite period at the end of her statement. She didn't want to be having this conversation because 1) Vicky was in a coma, 2) Vicky was supposedly talking to her in her dreams, 3) It was something spooky weird, and of course, she was supposed to know something about it, but in reality, she didn't have a clue what was going on, and 4) Cy was totally dating the cheerleader. "And stop trying to wheedle out of studying by researching ghosts and goblins."

"Ooh, do you think it's a goblin?"

Mary groaned.

~ ~ ~

"Ask Mr. Fletcher."

Mary ignored Rachel and read the next index card. "In humans, primary oocytes are located in the--?"

Rachel ignored her back. "Ask him."

"Answer the question."

"Ovaries. Ask him."

She put the cards down and looked at the ceiling. They were in the microfilm section. It was deserted because no one used microfilm if they didn't have to. "Mr. Fletcher, are you here?"

She waited for an acknowledgement. Nothing happened. Rachel could tell she didn't get a response. "Hey, Mr. Fletcher! We got a research question!"

"Rach!"

The living librarian stuck her head around the corner. "Do you girls need help?"

Mary was shaking her head when Rachel said, "Yes, ma'am. Can you show us how to get information about patients at the hospital?"

The librarian strolled back to them so Rachel wouldn't continue shouting across the room. This was supposed to be a quiet area. "You want patient information?"

"Yes," she said. She rolled her eyes a little. Mary wanted to kick her.

The librarian, whose name tag said Elizabeth, took Rachel's response in stride. "I'm afraid patient information is very sensitive. The hospital only gives that out to the patient, close family, or to someone with a court order. What exactly are you trying to find?"

"How many coma patients are at the hospital?"

Elizabeth blinked. "I'm sorry, girls, but that sort of information won't be available."

"How about, how many coma patients died at the hospital?"

She shook her head. "I'm really sorry. But

that kind of hospital specific information is not available. I could maybe find you national numbers if you're interested in those?"

Rachel shook her head. "Thanks, but we were interested in only the local hospital. We'll surf the net for something else."

Elizabeth nodded. "Well, just get me if you need any help."

When the librarian was gone, Rachel sighed and propped her chin on her fists. "I suppose Mr. Fletcher didn't show up while we were talking to her, did he?"

"No. We should get back to studying. That *is* why we're here."

Rachel made a face, but couldn't deny her statement.

"What is found in both prokaryotic and eukaryotic cells?"

Rachel stared into space. Mary waited for her to answer. While she waited, she flipped the card and looked at the answer. Rachel still didn't appear ready to answer.

"It starts with an 'R'."

Rachel straightened with enlightenment. "Mom!"

"What?" She didn't follow.

"I can ask her how many coma patients there are. Come on, I gotta get home." She stood and slung on her book bag.

"But what about studying?"

"I'm good. I haven't gotten one wrong, have I?"

Mary looked at the small stack of cards that they'd gone through and the much larger stack still in her hands. "Rach, you're procrastinating."

"No, you're avoiding your duty."

"What?"

"You have to help Vicky, but because she's like spite incarnate and dating Cy, you don't want to help her, so you're dragging your feet when you should be marching around this library asking for Mr. Fletcher."

Mary narrowed her eyes. "What's found in both prokaryotic and eukaryotic cells?"

Rachel screwed up her mouth.

She flipped to the next card. "When hydrogen ions are pumped out of the mitochondrial matrix, across the inner mitochondrial membrane, and into the space between the inner and outer membranes, the result is what?"

Rachel crossed her arms and stared her down.

"Are you not answering because you won't or because you don't know the answer?"

Rachel lifted her chin.

She flipped to another card. "What possesses a microtubular structure similar in form to a basal body?"

She watched Rachel closely. She still stood defiant, but there was uncertainty around her eyes. Mary lowered the flash cards. "Maybe the reason I'm not all gung-ho to help Vicky is because I don't know the answers either."

"I know the answers," Rachel muttered.

"Prove it."

Rachel turned her nose away, but she did sit back down.

"What possesses a microtubular structure similar in form to a basal body?" Mary repeated.

Rachel rocked a little in her seat.

"It starts with a 'C'."

She rocked more.

"I can't give you anymore hints because, frankly, I have no idea what this question is talking about."

She waited for her to reply, but Rachel was in one of her monumentally stubborn moods. Mary sighed and pushed the cards toward her. "Look, what I need to know will not be in any book or newspaper. I have to go to the hospital and walk around if I'm going to get any idea about what is hurting Vicky, but the hospital isn't going to just let us snoop. We need to enter the volunteer program, and the only way you're going to get into the program is if you ace this test, so let's get studying. All right?"

Rachel worked her jaw a bit but finally said,

"Centrioles."

She glanced at the note card. The answer was correct.

Rachel looked over at her with a small grin. "You know, we're going through an awful lot of trouble for Vicky."

"Don't remind me. Focus on all of the other nameless patients that we might be helping."

"Yeah, it's too bad none of them contacted you in your dreams for help. Does this mean she has, like, psychic ability?"

Mary shuddered as she recalled her first dream. "I hope not. A psychic Vicky would be terrible. Now no more Vicky talk. What is the function of water in photosynthesis?"

CHAPTER 4

Mr. Poopy-Pants

Mary and Rachel stumbled out of the library as it was closing at 7 p.m. They'd gone through the note cards twice. Rachel had gotten most of them right. "You're going to ace this test," Mary told her.

"Yeah, now let's celebrate."

"Celebrate?"

"Yeah, me acing the test."

"Um, I don't think you're supposed to celebrate something until after it happens."

"Really? What about baby showers and bridal showers? Let's have a test-acing shower."

"Why are those things called showers?"

"I guess because you get showered with gifts?"

"Huh."

Rachel began to bounce. "Let's go to The Drowsy Poet."

Mary's nose wrinkled. "It's Open Mic Night,

isn't it?"

"Maybe."

She winced. "I don't like listening to therapy sessions put to verse."

"Oh, come on, please? It's my Test-Acing Shower."

She sighed. Rachel had really buckled down while they were studying. She deserved some reward for that. "All right, but a dozen haikus or one sestina is my limit. Understand?"

Rachel nodded and happily skipped to the car. Mary really didn't understand her enjoyment of bad poetry, but then again, Mary didn't really have much tolerance for poetry, period.

It was a short drive to The Drowsy Poet. It was a small café-- with hopes of being a hip, artistic hangout--nestled in the corner of a shopping center. Abstract art done by local artists hung on the walls with price tags attached. There were tables with lounge chairs, high stools at the bar, and a few sofas pushed against the walls. The lighting was dim. A few groups of young people varying from high school to graduate school age were scattered around the room.

As she had dreaded, the small stage was lit, with a mic stand set up. As they went to the counter to place their orders, she looked around and spotted something new. There were some Internet terminals set up along the back wall.

Rachel ordered an iced chai latte and went to grab a seat on a sofa while Mary lingered a moment to ask the barista about the Internet terminals.

"They're five dollars an hour."

She paid and got the login information. She went over to Rachel.

"It looks like they're about to start," Rachel said, settling deeper into the sofa. Mary glanced toward the stage. There was a balding guy with a ponytail shuffling some note cards at the mic. She wished she had earplugs.

"I bought some time on one of the computers to look up some stuff. I'll be right over there."

Rachel's brow knitted. "We could've done that at the library."

"No, we were studying. I'm willing to take part in your test acing shower, but I'm gonna need some distraction. Now listen to emo guys wax tragically about their overbearing mothers and cheating ex-girlfriends while I surf the 'net."

"Can't you wait until you get home?"

"It'll be too late by then. I won't take too long."

"How much time did you buy?"

"How long will this be?"

Rachel frowned. "If you gave it a chance—" she started.

"I know, but I already bought the time."

Rachel glowered at her, but Mary couldn't muster much guilt. She settled down at the nearest computer terminal and logged in.

She pulled up Google and stared at the search box for a moment. Vicky really hadn't given her anything to go on. She typed in "claw soul" and hit enter. Nothing useful came back, though she was surprised by the number of Pokémon results. Did people still watch Pokémon? She returned to the search box. She typed in "bad ghost" this time. The results were a little better. She focused on reading personal accounts to see if anyone had a similar experience to what Vicky had described. She wasn't interested in the paranormal investigators because they relied on equipment she didn't need, and their results were usually false. She couldn't help snickering whenever anyone mentioned EVPs. How could anyone think a ghost's voice would appear on a recording device? And the recordings--she'd listened to some of those clips over and over again and could not hear the "words" the investigators were adamant were on them. It was static or background noise, nothing else. Among the personal accounts, there were a few that sounded similar to what Vicky described, but they were mostly one-time occurrences, not repeated attacks by the same entity.

"Whatcha reading?" Rachel had come up behind her and now leaned over her shoulder. Mary had been ignoring the poetry readings so hard that she'd missed her friend's approach.

"First-hand ghost stories, trying to figure out what's attacking Vicky."

"Find anything?"

"Not really. I mean some stuff is sort of similar but not entirely. I really need more info on what's happening at the hospital."

"So you want Vicky to bug you more in your dreams?"

She rolled her eyes at the possibility. She closed all the windows and logged off the computer. A short, chubby girl with violet hair was on the stage. She seemed to be just saying random words with weird pauses between them. She was really irritating. "Have you gotten your fill of poor-me-etry?"

"Don't call it that, and yeah, that last guy's diatribe about fat-free yogurt gave me a lot to think about."

Mary looked at her askance. "Please don't share your thoughts."

~ ~ ~

The bell to start sixth period had just rung, but Mary hadn't noticed. The world had shifted a little, and she was still thrown off by it. Cy was across the room. The seat beside her was empty. She was so used to seeing him beside her during English that seeing him elsewhere was playing with her spatial perception. He was sitting by Vicky's old seat, which everyone was still leaving empty. She was beginning to wonder if it had a bronze plaque dedicating it to her. He'd gone directly over to it without even a word to her. He'd said something to one of the girls sitting close by, and she'd nodded her head eagerly. It looked like Mary wouldn't be Xeroxing her notes for him that day. Maybe her handwriting had been too sloppy. More likely he didn't want to sit by someone who didn't like his girlfriend. Girlfriend. The word made her want to hurl.

She put on mental blinders during class and wouldn't let her eyes stray between Mrs. Myers and her notes. She would only look at one or the other. No straying side to side. She thought she caught in her peripheral vision a sandy haired head turned in her direction a couple of times, but she wouldn't let her pupils deviate from their strict path of teacher and notes. She was here to learn. She was determined to learn. Maybe she'd make honor roll this quarter. She should focus on school more anyway. It would serve her well later in life. Better than silly friendships that couldn't take a bit of snarking or disagreement. She may have ripped through her note paper a couple of times due to the zeal of her note taking, but it only showed her dedication to learning. She was sure of it.

When the final bell rang, she began collecting her things. She was getting picked up by Gran to go to Mrs. Beadley's home. They were going to see what they could do about her late husband.

"Hey, Mary."

Her notebook slid to the floor rather than into her bag. She looked up in surprise. "Kyle? Hey, what's up?"

He knelt down and retrieved her notebook. "Just collecting the invalid. You doing okay?"

She took the notebook and carefully put it into her bag. "I'm fine. Any news on Vicky?"

Kyle's brow furrowed at her question. She'd be surprised, too, if she were him, but she hadn't had a dream about the cheerleader the previous night, and she was a little worried. She hated that she was worried and wouldn't admit to it under torture, but there it was. "No change. I don't think the docs know what to do with her."

Cy came up to them but hung back a step. "I'm ready to go."

"That's great. Why don't you go wait by the truck?"

"Come on, Kyle. Mom told you to bring me straight home. I need to take my pain medication."

"You can wait five minutes."

Cy rolled his eyes and left the room. He hadn't even acknowledged her. She kept her eyes down as she got up and prepared to leave too.

"Hard to believe I'm the bad one," Kyle said.

"What?" She didn't know what he was talking about.

His mouth twisted, and he wouldn't meet her eyes. "Oh you know how it is with brothers. One's the good son, and other's the bad. The golden boy and the screw-up. I'm the screw-up."

"No, you're not. You do sports, are pretty popular, and don't pick fights and stuff. You're like all-American. Don't parents like that?"

"Yeah, but Cy's always been the center of attention. He has that stupid smile which everyone likes. They'll bend over backwards for him, and he doesn't have to do a thing."

Thinking about it, Mary couldn't really deny it, but she thought Kyle was being too hard on himself. From what she saw, he did just as well as Cy. She looked toward the door. She didn't really know how to end the conversation. She didn't want to just walk away, but Gran was waiting.

"Like right now, you think I shouldn't be making him wait for me. You think I should rush down and drive him home so he can take his precious pill while all evening Mom waits on him hand and foot, even though he can go to the kitchen and get his own stupid sodas."

She was shaking her head and leaning away from him before he was done. Kyle was getting kind of intense, and it was giving her unhappy flashbacks. While he was possessed, he'd cornered her in the hallway and threatened her. She'd been alone, and he'd scared her pretty bad. He was bigger and stronger, and she knew he could hurt her. Trying to keep her cool, she said, "No, it's just that Gran's waiting for me, and I don't want us to be late."

"Late for what?"

"An appointment. We're meeting a client."

"Well then, let's go." He stepped back and motioned her to go. She skirted around him and tried to keep from jogging out of there. It was tough to keep from going faster when Kyle fell into step beside her.

"So what are you going to do? An exorcism or something?"

Her eyes darted around the hall to see who was listening, but the place was pretty deserted. Everyone had left with the bell. "No, there's this widow whose dead husband is haunting her, and she wants our help with him."

She sneaked a look at Kyle. He seemed to be mulling that over. She wasn't sure if she should've told him all of that, but he was making her nervous, and she'd blabbed without thinking.

"Sorry for venting all over you."

"What?" She was beginning to get whiplash from his sudden turns in conversation.

"I know you're still sort of friends with Cy. I shouldn't have said all that stuff to you."

"No, it's okay. Everyone needs to just open up once in a while, right?" She hoped her smile was a friendly one, but it may have had more in common with a wince.

They'd reached the school doors. She quickly scanned the parking lot for Gran. A couple of horn toots helped find her. Kyle also looked in that direction.

"Geez, I hope I didn't keep you too long. Tell your grandma sorry for me."

"Yeah, sure." She took a few steps and stopped. She turned back. "Kyle, the reason people may not fall over themselves to help you is because you don't seem to need the help. I mean you seem really strong and together. People might think that they'd offend you or something if they offered. It doesn't mean they don't want to or whatever."

His shoulders relaxed, and he smiled at her. "Yeah, maybe. Thanks."

"Kyle, come on!"

Both turned to see Cy standing beside a pickup in the senior parking lot. He looked pretty impatient. For some reason, it made her smile.

"Bye, Kyle. See you around."

"Yeah, you too."

She left him and made her way to Gran in the station wagon. She opened the passenger side door and stopped. Sitting in the seat was Chowder's body. His ghost was there too, of course.

"What's he doing here?"

"I thought he might help."

"How?" She tossed her backpack onto the backseat and put Chowder on her lap, both physically and spiritually.

Gran shrugged and backed out of the spot. "I thought maybe he could sniff out the anchor."

Mary was skeptical that the little dog would be useful, but she kept it to herself. She looked at the top of his head. He was 'in' his body. He did that if he was being held. She gave him a scratch behind the ears. He gave a happy pant but finished it with a little whine. She wasn't sure what he could be begging for, but she figured it out after a second as she looked out the window. She rolled it down and stuck his head out. The wind blew his fur back, but that was all that moved on him. Gran couldn't stop laughing at the sight, but she couldn't hear his happy panting or feel his squirming glee. He was enjoying every second of the car ride. As she patted his back, she realized Chowder was very spoiled.

Mrs. Beadley's home was at the end of a quiet cul-de-sac. The front yard was tidy with pretty flower boxes lining the walkway. Mary followed Gran up the path. She had Chowder cradled to her chest. He panted happily against her face. He was still in his body. The whole day was turning out to be a real treat for him, but if he tried to lick her face one more time, she was going to put him back in the car and not leave a window cracked.

Mrs. Beadley was waiting for them. She waved, and Gran waved back like they were eagerly expected friends coming for a visit. Mrs. Beadley wore saucer-sized glasses with bright blue frames. Her white hair was tightly curled, and her head came up to Mary's shoulders.

"Mrs. Dubont, hello!" Mrs. Beadley smiled and held the door open for them.

"Hello to you, Mrs. Beadley. How are you?"

"Fair. He's been rather quiet. I think he knows how displeased I am and is hiding like a sullen, little boy."

"Well, I'd like you to meet my granddaughter Mary. She's very sensitive to ghosts."

Mrs. Beadley adjusted her glasses to better peer at her. "Oh how nice, and who is that you've got there?" Mrs. Beadley reached out as if to pet Chowder.

She held him up. "This is our dog. We're hoping he can help, too." Mrs. Beadley's hand stopped short of touching him. Her face froze, and she slowly drew her hand back as she realized that Chowder was a stuffed dog.

"How will he help?" Her voice cracked, and she coughed to clear it.

"We're hoping he'll sniff out your husband's anchor."

"Sniff out?"

"He's a ghost, too," Gran supplied.

Mrs. Beadley nodded, but it was clear she was having difficulty handling all of this. They may have sprung too much weirdness on her. "What do you need to do?" Mrs. Beadley asked.

Seeing her discomfort, Gran went to her side and put a comforting arm around her shoulders. "We're just going to try and talk to him today. That's all."

Gran looked over at Mary and tilted her head toward the living room. Mary stepped into the room and quickly scanned it. She couldn't feel anything, but that didn't mean Mr. Beadley wasn't lurking about. She set Chowder down and whispered, "Go find the ghost." She felt Chowder leave his body, which made her hands tingle. She imagined he was sniffing around like a dog would do. She had no clue if he'd understood what she'd asked or if he was just exploring.

She looked back at Gran and shrugged her shoulders to indicate that she wasn't picking up anything. Gran guided Mrs. Beadley into the room and helped her into a cushioned chair. She drew another up for herself and gently took the woman's hands.

"Tell me again about the last incident."

Mrs. Beadley nodded. "Okay. What happened was, Neil Connor came by to fix a short in the chandelier." She raised her eyes briefly to the lights overhead. "To thank him, I fixed dinner. Meatloaf. He said it was really good."

"Nobody fixes it better than you, Nina." The man's voice came from within the room, but Mary had no sense of his location. She touched Gran's shoulder and motioned for her to keep the woman talking.

"What happened?" Gran asked.

"We'd just sat down when every light in the house started to flicker. Neil went to check the panel. He's a very nice man."

"That's not what Gladys used to say. She was always saying that he didn't do his part around the house. You're too good for him." Gran had picked up a few of Mr. Beadley's words.

"He seems to think that Neil isn't good enough for you."

71

"Where would he get such an idea? Neil was his friend."

Mary spoke up, "Gladys was always complaining about him."

Mrs. Beadley's mouth dropped open. "Gladys? That was Neil's wife's name! How did you know that?"

Gran answered, "Your husband mentioned her. I think Gladys made him think Neil isn't good enough for you." She shot Mary a quick look to confirm what she'd said. Mary nodded.

"Well that's silly. Gladys, God rest her soul, was always a bit of a complainer. Neil was good to her and their kids. Marvin, you're not being fair."

Mr. Beadley didn't respond. "What happened next with Neil?" Gran prompted.

"He went to the electrical panel to check the breakers. Nothing was wrong, of course. He came back, and we started to eat. No sooner had he lifted the first forkful to his mouth when his glass of tea tipped over and spilled. We didn't see anything knock it over. It just tipped over on its own. It soaked his trousers. He mopped it up the best he could, but they weren't fit to wear. I offered him an old pair of Marvin's. He changed into them, and we tried to eat again. Only now the food was cold. I don't mean it had cooled off from sitting out. It was literally frozen. Neil looked at me, and I can only imagine what he thought. And it wasn't just the meatloaf: everything had been frozen. The mashed potatoes, the green beans, and the biscuits were all frozen. I can't believe Marvin would do that to me. It was so embarrassing."

"Then?" Gran asked.

"Then he took her out to dinner, and she didn't come home until eleven o'clock!" Mary winced at Mr. Beadley's exclamation. He had a very strident voice.

"He took me out to dinner. It was lovely. We talked for hours and laughed so hard our sides ached. I had a wonderful time."

Mary looked over at Gran and shrugged her shoulders. She really didn't know how to proceed with this. Didn't cops say domestic disputes were the most difficult calls to respond to? She was beginning to understand why. They both agreed on what happened but had differing reactions.

Gran stood up and moved to the center of the room. "Marvin, my name's Helena Dubont. Your wife has asked for my help. You can't go on haunting her like this. You both need to move on."

"Move on? What's there to move on to? Nina's my world."

"There is a place beyond this. You'll join your

parents and friends that have gone before you. You won't be alone."

"Who will look after Nina? Who'll help her?"

Gran turned to Mrs. Beadley. "He's scared to leave you because he thinks you'll be alone."

Mrs. Beadley looked down at her lap. "It's true that I don't have any close family to rely on. We weren't blessed with children."

Mary felt sorry for her. She looked to Gran and had to consider the fact that Gran was all the family she had. If she lost her...Mary didn't want to consider it. It was just too bleak.

"I would be okay, though. I'm not completely alone. Our friends have helped me. They've been so kind and generous."

"And Neil. He's falling all over himself being 'kind and generous.'" Gran and Mary ignored Mr. Beadley's snide remark.

"He's being a Mr. Poopy-pants right now, isn't he?" asked Mrs. Beadley.

Mary's eyebrows crept up, as she and Gran turned to look at her. Mrs. Beadley smiled and shrugged her shoulders. "You have the look. He's being a Mr. Poopy-pants." Her eyes got shiny, and she ducked her head. "I used to give him the same look."

"Oh, Nina. I'm never going to leave you. I'm not going anywhere."

Gran went to comfort her. Mary felt uncomfortable standing there. She wandered out of the room wondering where Chowder had gotten to. She went through the dining room and into the kitchen.

"Chowder?" she called softly, not wanting to disturb Gran and Mrs. Beadley. She heard a bark from inside the kitchen and looked around a bit. It was nice and clean. She closed her eyes and took a deep breath, trying to sense the anchor.

Another bark broke her concentration. She opened her eyes and looked around the floor. A cabinet door shook. "Is the anchor in there?" she asked. She opened the cabinet and looked inside. Pots and pans were stacked up inside. She reached inside to pull some of them out to sort through, but Chowder grabbed her sleeve and tugged.

"What is it, boy?"

Another cabinet door began to rattle. She closed the one she'd opened and reached for it, but the one she closed began to rattle again. She paused to think. Her eyes wandered to the overhead cabinets. She moved to open the one directly over the first cabinet.

"Mary, it's time to go."

She pulled the cabinet open and found glasses and coffee mugs.

"Your grandmother is calling you. Are you thirsty?"

She felt like she'd been caught snooping, which maybe she had been, but she was supposed to be, wasn't she? She closed the cabinet. She gave Mrs. Beadley a guilty look, made worse by the fact that the widow's eyes were red rimmed. "I was, but if we're leaving, it doesn't matter."

Gran appeared behind Mrs. Beadley. She had Chowder under her arm. "There you are. Let's go." Mary nodded and slipped by Mrs. Beadley. Gran gave the widow a hug and said she'd call her in two days but that Mrs. Beadley shouldn't hesitate to call her if she wanted to.

Mary didn't know what to say during the car ride home. She was totally out of her depth. Being haunted by a spouse, someone who'd spent decades with you, had to be conflicting. Having that someone there but not there had to be a hard thing to handle. But what about not having them there at all? She glanced over at Gran and wondered how she was feeling about all of this. Grandpa had passed away when Mary's mother was eight. He'd had a heart attack. There were pictures of him throughout the house, along with pictures of Mary's parents. She'd been four when her parents were killed. As awful as that had been, it was sort of abstract to her. She only had fuzzy memories of them. She knew stuff about them, but she didn't remember them. She

didn't really know what it felt like to lose someone. Had the visit brought up those feelings for
Gran? Was she missing them? Did Gran wish
her loved ones haunted her? She turned to ask
her but was cut off by Gran's excited announce-
ment.

"Oh, look. I think I have a new client."

Mary swallowed her question. Maybe she really didn't want to know.

CHAPTER 5

Volunteering to Help

Mary peered out the windshield to where Gran pointed. An old man stood beside a dark sedan parked off their driveway. He was dressed in slacks and a dress shirt with the cuffs rolled up. He perked up as Gran pulled in.

As they got out of the car, the man walked up. He seemed a little nervous and embarrassed to be there. It was a common thing with new clients, especially the ones with ghost problems.

"Sorry to bother you ladies, but are you Mrs. Dubont?"

Gran shut her door and reached out her hand. "Yes, I'm afraid these aren't my usual office hours. I'll be happy to make an appointment for you."

The man shook her hand lightly as if unused to shaking women's hands. "I understand, but I wanted to stop by because Nina Beadley told me about you."

"Mrs. Beadley?"

He nodded. "My name's Neil Connor, and I was hoping you could help me. I've got the same problem as Nina."

Gran shared a quick look with Mary. "The same problem?"

Mr. Connor stuck his hands in his pockets and looked at his shoes. "Yeah, and I think it's about time I got some help with it."

"Mr. Connor, just so there's no confusion, what exactly is it that you'd like me to help you with?"

Mr. Connor pursed his lips and nodded his head. "Fair enough, I'll have to come out and say it sooner or later. My problem is that I'm a widower, and my wife's still with me."

"Gladys?" Mary blurted out before she could stop herself.

Mr. Connor looked at her in surprise. "Yeah, that's my late wife's name. How'd you know? Are you psychic, too?"

Mary hugged Chowder. "Not psychic."

Gran quickly stepped in. "I'll be happy to make an appointment with you, Mr. Connor. Why don't you follow me, and we'll discuss it?"

Gran led Mr. Connor into her office while Mary went to the front to get the mail. She was still processing the coincidence of two people dating and both having ghostly-spouse problems. Was that how they had hooked up? Did they strike up a conversation one night while playing bridge and figure it out? 'My wife, God rest her soul, has been driving me crazy by turning on the radio at all hours of the night.' 'Oh, I know what you mean. My late husband likes to flick the lights. It's about to give me seizures.' 'Hey, you know what? We should go out. That'll drive'em crazy.' 'Yes, that'll be a switch.' And a happy couple was born from ghostly problems. Too bad relationships didn't usually work that way. Having ghost problems certainly hadn't brought her and Cy together.

When she got inside, she set Chowder down and tossed the mail onto the coffee table. She took her book bag upstairs to her room, and when she came back down, she found Gran in the kitchen with her head in the fridge.

"Did you and Mr. Connor figure something out?"

"Yes, we set up a meeting for next week. He told me a little bit about his situation, and it's surprisingly like Nina's."

"Huh, that's weird, isn't it?"

"Yes, but maybe we could use it to our advantage."

"How?"

"I'm thinking if the late Mr. Beadley and the late Mrs. Connor meet, they might be able to see that they're leaving their spouses well cared for.

Mr. Connor thinks he knows what his wife is anchored to, but he's been unable to part with it. I'm going to meet him at Nina's home and hopefully have a nice chat with all of them. Did Chowder find the anchor?"

"Yeah, I almost had it before we left. It's in the kitchen in one of the upper cabinets."

"That's good. Maybe I'll take him with me when I go back."

"Do you want me to come along?"

Gran shook her head. "No, I should be able to handle this by myself. You have school work and your volunteering to take care of."

"Yeah, but I like helping you."

Gran smiled. "I know, but this is my responsibility. Don't worry about it. Now I need to get dinner made, so we aren't late to your orientation."

~ ~ ~

"Which one are we signing up for again?" Rachel whispered.

"The hospitality cart."

"You know that means you're supposed to smile and chat with people, right?"

"Yeah, so?"

Rachel gave her a look.

"I can smile and chat."

She continued her look.

"Okay, I can smile. You can chat."

"Why do I have to be the Chatty Cathy?"

Mary threw Rachel's look right back at her.

"Fine, I'll chat, but you better smile so much your cheeks ache tomorrow."

She nodded and tried on a smile to show her acceptance of the plan. They'd listened to the volunteer coordinator tell them about how important patient confidentiality was and how they were supposed to be sensitive to the patient's needs and situation. They weren't supposed to make assumptions about the patient, and they weren't to pity the patients. It all sounded like good advice. They got their pictures taken for their ID badges, and they went over a map of the hospital. The coordinator told them what volunteers were expected and not expected to do like they could give patients a glass of water, but not help them to the bathroom. Finally, they were split up to start doing their new tasks.

Rachel and Mary were handed over to Mabel, a seasoned volunteer and retired nurse. She had short gray hair and big red lips. She beamed at them when they were led over, and crowed, "Yay! I get the young ones!"

Mary and Rachel gave her nervous smiles. Mabel's eyes softened. "It's really good to see two young ladies helping out. You two will be covering the second floor." When Mary heard that, she exchanged a quick glance with Rachel. They'd see Vicky.

Mabel showed them where everything was on the cart and how to fill the coffee and hot-water dispensers. Coffee, tea, magazines, and weekly newspapers were offered at no cost. Patients could also purchase small items from the cart, such as candy, toiletries, and stamps. They had to keep a tally of items sold and take special care with the cash box.

It all seemed simple enough except for the stopping and chatting bit. They were warned not to stay too long with a patient while on their rounds, but not to be in too much of a hurry either. If they wanted, they could promise to come back once their rounds were done to sit with patients and play board games or cards.

"That would really delight some of these guys. If you need a board game, just ask at the nurse's station. They usually have a few stowed there."

Mary was starting to feel really nervous. She hadn't signed up to really volunteer, just to snoop, but here was Mabel saying that they could do someone a lot of good by playing a round of Pictionary. It seemed mean not to be willing to do that.

Mabel led them around the second floor.

Mary got stuck pushing the cart while Rachel knocked on doors to ask if anyone wanted anything.

There were a few requests for coffee. Mary filled cups and helped Rachel take them in. Mabel introduced them to patients and nurses. A lot of the nurses knew Rachel's mom so were extra-welcoming. Mary was starting to get dizzy from all the nodding and hello-ing. Everyone was just so happy to see them. It was making her a bit nauseated.

She wasn't sure if she could go into Vicky's room when they came to it. She was nervous about who she'd find in there. Rachel glanced at her, and she could see the nervousness in her eyes, too. Mabel was oblivious to their tension. She motioned for Rachel to knock. Rachel tapped softly on the door and opened it a crack.

"Would anyone like something from the hospitality cart?" she asked. Mary couldn't see into the room, but from the way Rachel worded the question, she knew there had to be multiple people in there. She hoped it was just Vicky's parents.

"Rachel?"

Nope, not just her parents.

"Hey Cy, I'm volunteering with the hospitality cart. Would you like anything from it? Would you, Mrs. Nelson?"

The door was pulled open wider, and Cy stood there. His eyes widened when he saw Mary. She grasped the handlebar to the cart tighter and twisted it a bit, ready to take off at a sprint with it.

"Oh, you know each other?" Mabel said.

"We know Vicky. She goes to our school," Mary said. She stared at Cy and then past him into the room. Mrs. Nelson came up behind him.

"Oh, you girls volunteer? That's really nice. I'm glad I get to see you again. I didn't catch your names when you were here earlier."

"Oh, um, I'm Rachel and that's Mary," Rachel said.

"Rachel and Mary. I think Vicky has mentioned a classmate named Mary…" Mrs. Nelson trailed off and then sort of jumped. Mary figured the only way Vicky would've mentioned her was in a disparaging manner. She had no idea how explicit Vicky would have been with her mother about her loathing of Mary but gaging from Mrs. Nelson's reaction, she'd been told a little at least.

Mrs. Nelson quickly composed herself and said, "I think I will take a cup of coffee."

Cy was glaring at Mary. She tried to ignore him, but her eyes kept jumping to him. She was jittery as she poured the coffee and spilled some over her hand. It made her hiss.

"Any change with Vicky?" Rachel asked. She handed the coffee to Vicky's mother.

She took a sip of her coffee and shook her head. "None, but there's still plenty of hope."

"We should be going. Don't want to bother you," Mary said.

"Please stop by again. It was nice meeting you both." Rachel and Mary gave Mrs. Nelson a polite nod. Cy still stood in the doorway, arms crossed, eyes locked on them. Mary avoided his eyes.

Once they were further down the hall, Mabel tentatively asked, "Is the young lady a good friend of yours?"

Rachel didn't answer. She appeared very engrossed in the floor tiles. Mary softened the truth so as not to upset Mabel. "Not really, but I've known her for years, and the guy that was there was a friend." She grimaced and hoped Mabel thought the past tense was a simple grammatical error, though the way he had scowled at them the whole time probably made her reasons for using the past tense pretty obvious. Mabel didn't reply. She just nodded her head.

They were walking through the last wing. Rachel had taken charge and was knocking on every door without prompting, but as she went to knock on one door, Mabel swooped in to stop her.

"This room doesn't need hospitality."

"It's empty?" Rachel asked because there appeared to be a chart on the door.

Mabel grimaced and opened her mouth to reply but didn't get a chance because from behind the closed door, a cranky, nasally voice shouted, "Don't you dare slide on by! I want coffee!"

Mabel's shoulders slumped. "Make up one cup of coffee. Black. I'll take it in. You girls can wait out here."

"What's wrong?" Rachel asked. The retired nurse had been so energetic and cheerful up until that moment.

"Mr. White is one of our more unpleasant patients. You don't have to stop by his room."

"Quit your old woman gossiping and bring me my coffee!"

Mabel's lips thinned. She muttered, "I'll bring you your coffee, you evil old goat." But when she pushed the door open, there was a smile on her face. Rachel and Mary raised their eyebrows at each other. They stole a peek into the room. An old man was propped up in one of the beds with a breathing tube looped across his face. The other bed was empty.

"That sure as hell better not be decaf," he said.

Mabel set the cup on his bed table. "No, it's full strength with a dash of arsenic for extra kick."

The old man harrumphed, and his eyes shot to the door. "Well, get your sorry asses in here if you want to take a gander. Can't see much of anything cowering like yellowbellies in the doorway."

The girls looked to Mabel for her nod before taking a few small steps in. "Young ones, eh? What'd you do to get this punishment? Crash Daddy's car while high on Mary Jane?"

"We're volunteering because we want to. Do you need anything else, Mr. White?" Rachel asked.

Mr. White ignored her question. He turned to Mary with a sly smile. "Like I'm supposed to believe *that* one's here on her own volition. Bet her skin's just crawling. Or ears burning. How's the heavenly choir sounding?"

She stiffened. How did he know? She stared at him harder, really looking at him. She looked past the breathing tube, the IV line, and the heart monitor. She looked at his arms and his hands. There were jeweled rings on his gnarled fingers, and dark inky tattoos on his forearms. The rings had sigils on them and the tattoos were pentagrams with various symbols and writing around them. Signs of power and protection. "Anything tugging at you, Mr. White? Pulling you down?"

Mabel looked startled by her question, but Mr. White only chuckled. "Ain't no shadows here, little girl."

CHAPTER 6

The Shadowman

After Mabel ushered them out of Mr. White's room, she told them that they didn't need to stop by his room ever again. Mary and Rachel nodded obediently, but Mary knew they would be going back. He was their only lead. They finished their shift and thanked Mabel for showing them everything. Once they were free of her, they went back to his room.

"Do you really think he knows something?" Rachel asked.

Mary shrugged. "He seemed to. He called me out clear enough."

"What if he's behind the thing harming Vicky?"

"I don't know about that. Why let on that he knew anything? I don't even know what's bothering Vicky. He has a clue." Mary knocked, but Mr. White didn't call them in.

She opened the door cautiously. He was still

propped up in his bed, but his eyes were closed and his mouth was hanging open. "Mr. White?" she called.

He didn't stir. They crept up to the bed. "Mr. White?" she called again. He still didn't stir.

"Do you think he's dead?" Rachel whispered.

"Do I look dead?" he snapped, opening his eyes to glare at her.

Rachel jumped. "Um, yeah?"

He smacked his lips and turned to Mary. "So you're here about the Shadowman."

"What's a Shadowman?"

"What you're after."

"But what is it?"

He just grinned.

Her eyes narrowed. "What do you know?"

Mr. White chuckled again and looked at his nails. "I know all sorts of things. Want a few things, too."

"You want us to bribe you?" Rachel asked.

He pointed at her. "She's quick. Can see why you keep her around."

"What do you want?" Mary asked, already getting a sinking feeling.

"Stuff that ain't on the hospitality cart. At least not yet. Gonna bring me a few things and then I'll tell you about the Shadowman."

"That thing's hurting people, and you're going to force us to bring you stuff before you help?" Rachel demanded.

"What I got to tell is valuable, isn't it? Can get stuff for it. Capitalism is a lovely thing."

"What do you want?" Mary repeated.

Rachel crossed her arms, clearly not happy to be even listening to the old man's demands.

"I want what any man wants: cigars, booze, and women. Get me a pack of Swisher Sweets, a bottle of JD, and a couple issues of *Hustler*."

"We aren't old enough to buy any of those things. We're not old enough to even touch them," Rachel said.

"Not my problem."

"How do you know about the Shadowman? How'd you know about me?" Mary asked.

"Can see it. How else?"

"What do you see?"

Mr. White stared at her a moment and then his eyes slid away. "Can just see ya, that's all."

"What about the Shadowman? What do you know about it? A classmate told me it was clawing at her. She thought it was going to kill her."

"Might do that. Better get me what I want quick, if you're going to stop it."

She stared at him. Frustration bubbled up in her. What he wanted was impossible. They couldn't get those things. She didn't even know where to get issues of *Hustler*. Like Rachel said, how could he demand these things when people were in danger? She wasn't asking Vicky for payback for helping her. Rachel tugged on her arm.

"Come on, Mary. Let's just go."

Mary followed Rachel out of the room. She took one last look at Mr. White before closing the door. He'd leaned back in his bed, and his eyes were closed once again.

"I can't believe that old fart. Asking us to get those things-- isn't that like corrupting a minor or something?"

"He knows something, Rach."

"Yeah, probably because he's the one behind it. He's our prime suspect. We should investigate him."

"How?"

"Mabel might know something. We should ask her. We're supposed to come back in two days for our next shift."

They were at the elevators again, waiting for a car. She didn't know what to make of Mr. White. She didn't suspect him, like Rachel did. He had the gift. She couldn't imagine someone with the gift doing wrong with it. She knew that was probably naïve, but she had to believe it. She'd been called evil before, but she knew that the ones who'd called her that were wrong. She was different, but that didn't mean she was evil, and the same went for Mr. White.

The elevator doors opened to reveal Cy, whose eyes narrowed when he saw them. Mary's stomach dropped, but Rachel wasn't as thrown off by his appearance. "Hi, Cy. Glad Vicky's doing okay." Rachel edged around him to get into the elevator, tugging Mary with her. Cy stepped in their way.

"What are you two doing here?"

"We finished up volunteering and are now going home. It was our first day."

"You just decided to start volunteering?" he asked. He sounded suspicious. She didn't know what he could be thinking. She doubted he'd consider the possibility that Vicky had visited her in a dream and asked for her help, and it wasn't like she could tell him that.

"Rachel's mom is a nurse. She encouraged us to volunteer. It'll look good on our college applications." The lie came out without any thought. A while back, she'd accepted the fact that she would have to lie to Cy to have any sort of relationship with him. She tried not to think about the fact that she needed to lie to a boy she liked to get him to like her. She suspected that by doing so, she was somehow lying to herself.

"Yeah, my mom's all about creating the stellar college application."

He crossed his arms and stared at the floor

for a bit before he spoke. "Look, don't mess with Vicky. I know she has never been your friend, but she's in a coma. That's bad. It's not some opportunity to get one up on her or something. Just leave her alone. A lot of people care about her, and we're all praying that she makes it through this. Just respect that, okay? Please?"

She didn't know what to say. He really thought this was just one big ploy to mess with Vicky? Her world didn't revolve around Vicky-- though currently she did affect the orbit some, but everything was NOT about Vicky. She suddenly knew what to say. "There are over a hundred patients in this hospital. Only one of them happens to be Vicky. We just spent the last two hours going around and helping some of them. We aren't here to mess with her. We're trying to help others. Get over yourself."

She stomped into the elevator and jabbed the "door close" button. Rachel slipped in behind her. Cy stared at them as the doors shut. His gaze was sad. She'd snapped at a guy who was worried about his hurt girlfriend. She needed to shake off the guilt that welled up. He'd deserved it, and she hadn't been that harsh. At least, she didn't think so. She wasn't going to apologize.

Rachel had pressed the button for the lobby, but when the elevator began to move, it rose.

"Darn, I didn't notice the elevator was going up," Rachel said.

Mary wasn't so sure. "What's going on?"

"The elevator was going up when we got on. Cy must have distracted us too much to notice."

Mary raised her hand with a shake of her head. "Where are you taking us?" she asked.

The elevator stopped, and the doors slid open, *"Go to room 308."*

"Why?"

The ghost didn't reply. Deciding to humor him, she got off, took a quick look at the room signs, and began going down the hall.

"Where are we going?" Rachel asked as she caught up.

"To room 308."

"Was there a ghost on the elevator?"

"Yeah, but he's not very chatty. He only told me the room number."

As they walked down the hallway, the florescent lights flickered and dimmed. The hallway was empty. No hospital staff was in sight. Rachel stepped closer to her. "Is it me, or has it gotten really creepy?"

Rachel was right. Something was wrong. They came to the room. The door was closed. She grabbed the door knob and turned. The door wasn't locked. It swung open to reveal a pitch-black room.

"This isn't right," Rachel said.

Mary flipped the light switch, and the room lit up. For a second, a dark shadow was draped over the unconscious patient. The shadow was humanoid like a person's shadow, except for two red eyes peering out from the head. When the lights came on, it slithered off the patient and under the bed. As if the light switch had also turned back on the medical equipment, alarms started going off. Remembering her training from only a few hours before, Rachel rushed to the bed and hit the "code blue" button.

Steeling herself, Mary dropped to her knees and looked underneath the bed, but the Shadowman was gone. She saw a ventilation grill on the bottom of the wall. It must have gone through that to escape.

Nurses and doctors rushed into the room and began helping the patient. Rachel's mother was one of them. "Girls, get back! What are you two doing in here?"

"We heard something and looked in. I hit the button because he wasn't breathing right," Rachel said.

"You did the right thing, but you two should leave now."

"Yes, Mrs. Pillar," Mary said.

As they walked back to the elevator, Rachel whispered, "Did we really just see that thing?"

She could only nod. She had no idea what that thing had been. Except for clairvoyants, people never saw ghosts. Ghosts couldn't make themselves visible, even if they were strong enough to move stuff. She'd never seen a ghost, though of course she'd heard plenty. But that thing hadn't been a ghost. The feeling she'd gotten from it was so strange. When it had looked at her, she knew that it had never been human. "We need to talk to Gran."

"About time," Rachel said.

~ ~ ~

Gran was watching TV with Chowder's body tucked beside her on the sofa when the girls arrived. She quickly shut off the TV when she saw their faces and gestured for them to take seats. "What happened?"

Mary sat down beside Gran, while Rachel sat on her other side. She took a deep breath to steel her nerves. She knew she should've told Gran about Vicky the moment she'd known that her dreams were more than dreams, but she hadn't wanted to burden her with it. But now, she didn't know what to do and needed help. Assuming she could do this on her own had been wishful thinking. She still didn't know much about the supernatural, and the only person she knew who did was Gran.

"Remember I told you about that girl from school who's in a coma?"

"Yes. Vicky, right? A friend of Cyrus's?"

Her mouth twisted as she kept herself from correcting Gran's misconception of the relationship. "Yeah, she's somehow communicating with me through dreams. She says she's in trouble and needs my help."

"How is she in trouble?"

"She thinks something supernatural is attacking her. That's why I signed up to volunteer at the hospital. I wanted to see if I could find out what could be hurting her. And I did find something out. I met a patient who seemed to know stuff. He said he'd tell me about what's doing this, but he wanted Rach and me to get him things that we can't get, like cigars, alcohol, and porno mags."

"Good Lord, who in blazes would ask that of teenage girls?"

"His name's Mr. White. I don't--"

"Ezekiel White?"

"I don't know his first name. He's an old man with white hair. He has the gift. He knew straightaway about me."

Gran nodded her head. "Ezekiel White."

"You know him, Mrs. Dubont?"

A faraway look came into Gran's eyes. "Yes,

at least I did a long time ago. He was a rare book dealer and occultist. His shop has been closed for years. I thought he'd retired and moved away."

"Tell her about the thing attacking coma patients," Rachel said.

"Mr. White called it a Shadowman."

Gran's eyes widened. "Are you sure? Is that exactly what he said?"

"Yeah, and we saw it. It was lying on top of a coma patient, not Vicky. When we turned on the lights, it left, but it was a black misty form with red eyes."

Gran shook her head and got up. "This is bad, girls. You two should not be dealing with this. Leave it to me. I'll talk to Ezekiel and work on removing the Shadowman. Don't worry about it anymore. Your friend will be fine."

"Gran, let us help."

"No, I'll take care of it. You both should probably not volunteer anymore until I've dealt with this."

"Gran--"

"I mean it, Mary. Do as I say. This is far too dangerous for you. You too, Rachel. Swear to me that you won't go to the hospital until I say it's safe."

"We swear, Gran. Just be careful."

"I'm always careful, dear. No need to worry

about me."

~ ~ ~

"So what have you found out?"

Mary would really like it when she could once again claim sleep as a Vicky-free zone. She turned to the girl in the hospital bed. "There is something supernatural attacking patients at the hospital, but I think if someone's with you, and you keep the lights on, you should be fine."

"Oh, that should be simple to manage. I'll just—Oh, whoops! I'm in a coma!"

"Don't worry. My grandmother is coming to deal with this thing. You'll be fine. She knows this stuff."

"Is your grandmother a real witch? I always thought so, but--"

"She's not a witch. She's a fortuneteller and a medium. She doesn't cast spells or perform ceremonies."

"Then what's she going to do?"

Mary didn't answer because she had no idea. She wished she'd gotten more information from Mr. White. Instead, she asked, "Has the Shadowman bothered you any since last time?"

"Not really. I've felt it sort of pass by a few times, but it hasn't come after me again."

"Probably because your mom and Cy are

with you."

"You saw my mom?"

"She seems nice. She really cares about you."

Vicky looked away. "Well, she is my mom."

"You're going to be okay."

Vicky kept her eyes turned away. There was a small furrow between her brows. "Even if this thing is taken care of, it doesn't mean I'll wake up."

"You don't know that."

"This thing didn't put me in the coma."

"But it might be what's keeping you in it."

"Thanks for helping me, Mary. And thank your grandmother. And I guess Rachel, also. She's been helping, hasn't she?"

"Yeah, she has."

"Then thank her, too."

Mary was uncomfortable with the way Vicky was talking. Why did anyone need thanking? They hadn't done anything yet. "You're going to be okay."

"Maybe, but if not, tell my parents that I love them, and tell Cy that he's a really great guy. I wish I'd had more time with him."

"No."

Vicky finally turned her head to her. "What do you mean 'no'?"

"I'm not telling your parents or Cy any of that. In fact, if you don't wake up, I'm going to tell them all sorts of horrible things. I've got plenty of stuff I could tell them, true stuff at that, and if you're not awake by the time I'm done, I'll start making stuff up. I'll lie, and you won't be able to stop me."

"You're bluffing. You wouldn't dare."

"Don't wake up, and you'll find out."

"I know what you're trying to do."

"And I know what you're trying to do, too. Oh, boohoo, you're in a coma. Let's all build a shrine to the poor, unfortunate cheerleader. Nuh-uh. I'll tear it down. I'll spray paint 'Vicky The Hickey' on it, burn all the flowers, and eviscerate the stuffed animals. You don't get to be a martyr."

"Yeah, and how am I supposed to stop you? How am I supposed to wake up?"

"I don't know, but you'll figure it out. You'd better. You don't want to leave me out here to do as I please, and I'll have Rachel to help me. It'll be fun."

Vicky glowered at her from the hospital bed. Mary stared back defiant. The dream snapped off like a phone being slammed. As she drifted back to normal sleep, Mary hoped she'd convinced Vicky not to give up.

~ ~ ~

Mary and Rachel were sitting together in the crafts classroom during TAB. Crafts was Rachel's next class.

"So what do you think Gran's going to do?"

Mary shrugged. "I have no idea. I wish she'd let me help her on this."

"Hey, Mary."

She looked up and saw Kyle. He came over to their table.

"Hey, what's up?"

"Heard you went by to see Vicky."

She rolled her eyes. "It wasn't a big deal. We were already there for something else."

Kyle sort of shuffled his feet and ducked his head. If he weren't a two-hundred pound wrestler, he'd have looked bashful. "I think it was pretty cool of you that you did. Not as many people as you'd think have been by to see her."

"Who has been by?" Rachel asked.

Mary threw her a look. Why'd she ask that? But Rachel wasn't paying attention to her. She'd opened a spiral notebook and had a pen ready.

"Well, my brother and I, obviously, her parents, Carolyn, Mary-Jo, and I think that's it, except for you two."

"Anyone else not from school or the hospital?" Rachel asked, writing down the names he'd given.

Kyle thought about it a moment and

shrugged. "No, I don't think so. Mrs. Nelson hasn't mentioned anyone else."

"What about Helen, Brittany, Gloria, Denise, Bobby, Trevor, and Harry?" Mary rattled off the names in surprise. Those were some of Vicky's posse. She figured they'd have gone by at least once to see her. Really, she figured half the school would have visited. She wouldn't have been surprised to find a bunch of them keeping vigil until the queen bee woke up.

Kyle shook his head. "I think the girls may have sent some flowers, but they haven't been by."

That news made Mary feel bad for Vicky, which put a nasty taste in her mouth. She may be in a coma and getting attacked by a Shadow-man, but to be abandoned by her supposed friends was the worst thing of all. "That sucks."

"Yeah, I think her mom isn't taking it well. I mean she knows how popular Vicky is, and for no one to be coming to see her, it's really bothering her."

"Have any of the medical staff been acting weird? Have any of them been overly attentive? Wait, not just medical staff but anyone else like volunteers or janitorial staff?"

Kyle squinted at Rachel. "I don't know. Why are you asking?"

Rachel scribbled a few words in her notebook and shrugged. "No reason. Just making conversation."

Kyle looked at Mary, clearly not buying Rachel's lie. Mary knew what her friend was doing, but she wasn't about to blab about it to him. Later, though, she'd make Rachel look up the word "subtle."

"Mary Hellick, please come to the principal's office."

Everyone in the room turned to look at her and made "Oooh" sounds, like little kids. "What'd you do?" Rachel asked.

Mary sighed as she picked up her book bag. "I have no idea. Bye, Kyle. Thanks for the info."

CHAPTER 7

Falling Down

As she walked to the principal's office, she tried to think of why she'd been summoned. Nothing was coming to mind. She hadn't done anything disruptive in over a month. She hadn't had any confrontations or pulled any pranks, which Rachel could attest to, since one of them never did a prank without the other.

Which reminded her, they really needed to do something. She'd have to think on it. She'd already decided to target the student government this time. They'd been harping on about some trip to D.C. and having bake sales, car washes, and donation drives to raise money. She'd taken special offense to the donation drive. Why should she give money to help buy plane tickets for kids who drove BMW's?

When she entered the principal's office, the secretary smiled at her. The way she smiled put her on guard. The secretary never smiled at her, and this smile wasn't a cheery smile. It was a pitying one. The secretary led her back to the office. Principal Hoke and Mr. Landa were inside. Principal Hoke and she had never met under pleasant circumstances, and this time looked to be no different. But she still didn't know what the unpleasantness was.

"Mary, please have a seat."

She sat down, but the two grown-ups remained standing. Principal Hoke had both her hands clasped before her, and Mr. Landa had his in his pockets, but their stances weren't relaxed. They looked stiff.

"Mary, there's been an accident."

At that statement, she went still. Goosebumps rose on her arms, and a shiver went down her spine. She was startled when Mr. Landa pulled a chair up beside her. She looked at him with wide eyes. He put a hand on her shoulder. "Your grandmother fell at the hospital. She's been admitted."

"Will she be all right?"

He patted her back. The contact made her shoulders tense up. "I'll give you a ride there." His non-answer made her tense up more.

"Mary, I'm very sorry. Let us know if there's anything we can do."

"Thanks, Ms. Hoke." In a slight daze, she stood and followed Mr. Landa out. The bell hadn't rung yet for next period. Students were milling about in the entryway. Mr. Landa guided her to the door. His hand was again on her shoulder. She wanted to shrug it off but couldn't bring herself to do it. What had happened to Gran?

"Mary!" She looked up at Rachel's call. She and Kyle were standing at the stairway entrance. Mr. Landa paused to let her speak to them. Rachel rushed up.

"What's going on?"

"Gran's been hurt."

"What?" She pulled Mary into a hug.

She put her arms around her, grateful for the comfort. "They say she fell. Mr. Landa's taking me to the hospital."

"Okay, I'm coming."

At that statement, Mr. Landa jumped into the conversation. "I'm sorry, Rachel, but you need to go to class."

She turned to glare at him. "I love her, too!"

"That may be, but I don't have permission to take you off school grounds. You can come by after school, during visiting hours."

"It's okay, Rach. I'll see you in a little while."

Rachel nodded and gave her another hug. "Don't do anything stupid until I get there," she whispered.

Mary nodded and hugged her again.

Her eyes met Kyle's over Rachel's shoulder.

He looked uncomfortable. She gave him a small smile. "Hope everything's okay," he offered.

She nodded. The bell rang. Mr. Landa began going to the main doors again. She followed behind to the staff parking lot. She didn't know what car he drove. She was surprised when the black Kia Amante's lights blinked. She'd figured him for a Chevy Corsair or maybe an Ugo.

She got into the passenger seat. "Thanks for giving me a ride," she said as she buckled her seat belt.

"It's no problem. I'm glad I can help. Do you know why your grandmother was at the hospital?"

"She was going to see an old friend. I met him while volunteering, and she was going to talk to him."

Landa nodded absently as he backed out. "How's volunteering?"

"It's okay. Everyone seems really nice."

"That's good. So you're friends with Kyle?"

She got the feeling that this was no longer a simple favor for her but a scheduled session. "Yeah, I guess. I'm friends with his brother, so I guess I'm friends with him."

"Vicky and Cyrus are close."

She slouched down in her seat and fixed her eyes on the windshield. Why did everyone feel the need to discuss this with her? "Yeah, they like each other."

"But you and Vicky have never gotten along."

"No, but we're doing okay now."

His eyes slanted to her. "Since she's been in a coma?"

She knew what he was thinking, but she wasn't being sarcastic. "Yeah, we talk all the time now."

He shook his head.

"I do want Vicky to get better. I may not particularly like her, but her parents and Cy care about her, so I want her to get better."

"That's good."

"Do you know anything about Gran?"

He didn't answer. She wanted to curl into a little ball. What had happened to Gran?

They arrived at the hospital in silence. Mr. Landa pulled up at the front. She opened the door and had one foot out when she turned back. "Thanks for the lift. I got it from here."

"Are you sure?"

She glanced toward the hospital. "I know the layout pretty well. I'll get the room number from information. I'm sure you need to get back to school. Mrs. Pillar is here if I need anything. Don't worry about me."

"I'm not worried. I just want to make sure that you're okay."

"Aren't those the same thing?"

He gave her a small grin. "A little. Will you be okay?"

"I'll be fine. Once I see Gran, everything will be okay."

He looked at her for a moment as if he were determining whether she was telling the truth. She was getting antsy. She wanted to get inside now. He finally nodded. "If you need anything, give me a call."

She nodded as she closed the door, and then strode into the hospital. Once she was inside, she faltered. What had happened to Gran? How was she? She wanted to know, but she was scared to find out. The hospital appeared no different than when she'd been there last night. Visitors and staff went about their business as usual, but it was different this time. Someone she cared about had been admitted. Her first stop was the information desk. The woman working there smiled sunnily at her. She couldn't return even a half smile. "Could you tell me what room Helena Dubont is in, please?"

She looked up the name in her computer. "She was put in room 224."

Mary recognized the room number and raised an eyebrow. She started for the elevators before the receptionist looked up from her computer screen.

The elevator was empty when she got on it. *"What floor, please?"*

"Two. Did the Shadowman attack my grandmother?" The button for two lit up, but the ghost didn't reply. "Do you know anything about what happened to my grandmother?"

Still the ghost didn't answer. Why wouldn't anyone tell her anything? She crossed her arms and tapped her feet.

"Second floor."

The elevator stopped and the doors slid open. "Thanks," Mary grumbled as she strode out. She quickly turned down the hall to room 224. As she arrived there and reached to open the door, raised voices stopped her.

"You are so full of it! Tolliver's book was a crock, and you know it!"

"He got the alignment right, didn't he?"

"Pure chance! He doesn't know his Manipura chakra from a bleeding ulcer!"

She pushed the door open slowly and peeked in. Gran was sitting up, with her left foot suspended over the bed. She looked flushed and ornery. Mr. White was rather rosy in the cheeks as well.

"Gran?"

"Mary! Oh no, I told the hospital not to call the school."

She went to the bed and stared at her suspended foot. It wasn't in a cast. It was in an ace bandage. The injury didn't make sense. "Did the Shadowman do this?"

"No, tell her what really happened!" Mr. White said.

She glanced at him and then back at her. "Gran?"

"Don't pay any attention to him."

"Did the Shadowman do this?"

"No, dear. I slipped. That's all. I sprained my ankle, and now I'm waiting on x-rays to see if I broke anything."

Mr. White snorted. "If you believe that, then instead of her foot, they should x-ray your head!"

"What's he talking about?"

"He has this crazy notion—-"

Mr. White shook his finger at her. "It is not crazy! You fell down those stairs on purpose!"

Gran rolled her eyes. "Yes, that sounds sane and sensible."

"I didn't say you were sane or sensible."

Mary didn't know what to believe. "Did the Shadowman do this?!"

"No!" They both shouted.

She threw up her hands. "Then what's going on?"

Gran's lips screwed up into a scowl. Mr. White, though, was more than eager to answer.

"Because I wouldn't tell her anything about that stupid Shadowman, she went and hurt herself so she could trap me and wear me down until I tell her what she wants to know. It's insane, and I'm not telling you a blasted thing!"

Mary turned to Gran hoping for a more sensible answer. "Gran, is that what happened?"

She lifted her chin and looked down her nose at her. There was a flintiness in her eyes that Mary knew very well. She couldn't believe it. Gran had totally done it on purpose. She'd twisted her ankle to trap and interrogate Mr. White. "Have you at least found out anything?"

"He's a stubborn old man."

"You're damn right, I am. You aren't getting anything out of me."

Gran cast a sideways glare at Mr. White that looked absolutely evil. He didn't know it yet, but he was in for trouble. "Mary, the doctors suggested I stay overnight for observation. I think I will. Be a dear and bring me a few things from home." The way she sweetly said it made Mary's eyes dart to Mr. White. He was in for it now. "Along with all the regular stuff, could you bring a few specials things? I'd like my CD player and my Dean Martin discs. He's such a wonderful singer. Listening to him will certainly lift my spirits. And did you notice that the television has a DVD player? Bring all of my Martin and

Lewis movies. We could have a marathon. Wouldn't that be fun? And finally, I'd really like to have my autographed picture of Dino with me. Holding it is such a comfort. Got that?"

Every time she mentioned Dean Martin, Mr. White's eye had twitched. The way Gran sounded, one would think she was a total Dean Martin fan girl, and Mary had known she liked him, but she didn't listen to his music much or watch the DVDs. She'd probably have to wipe dust off them before bringing them in.

"I'll give you fifty bucks to disobey your grandmother."

She turned to Mr. White. This could get interesting. "Thanks, but I don't want money."

"A hundred dollars."

"You know what I want."

"Two hundred."

"Zeke," Gran said in a chiding tone.

"I'm going to get something for my information. You're not getting it free."

"You will get something--a Dino-free zone." Gran had him. She had the same look in her eyes as when a client blustered about paying for her services. She'd get them to pay--and tip well, too.

Mr. White worked his jaw. Gran started humming the tune for "That's Amore."

"Bwah! Fine! You want to know about

Shadowmen? I'll tell you. They're nasty. They glom onto people and feed off of them. People hardly ever know they're victims. They just feel worn down and surly. Usually, the Shadowman will leave them on its own for a new victim."

"How do you get rid of them?" Mary asked.

Mr. White shrugged.

"What?"

"I don't know how to get rid of them. People have tried blessings and exorcisms, but nothing seems to definitively work. No one knows what they are. They don't seem like ghosts. They aren't demons. They're a nuisance. That's all anyone is sure of."

"But this one's attacking people in the hospital. It may be killing them. That's way more than a nuisance."

"I remember you saying that, and I don't understand it, but then again, nobody really understands Shadowmen. They just are."

She looked at Gran to get her take on this. She was tapping a finger against her lips, obviously thinking. "There has to be a way to help Vicky," Mary said to her.

Gran nodded. "Zeke, have you seen the Shadowman that's here? Has it tried to sneak into your room?"

Mr. White hunched over. "Yeah, it has, but I was always able to send it packing."

"We need to lure it out and then follow it. Mary, I need you to go home and get Chowder and all the flashlights."

"What are you planning?"

"We need to track it. Figure out where it rests. I think that will tell us how to get rid of it."

"What do you mean lure it out? Are you going to make yourself vulnerable to this thing?" Mr. White sounded concerned. It made alarms go off in Mary's head, too.

"I don't like this plan much either, but if we hope to stop this entity, we need to find where it rests and anything else we can about it."

"How are you going to track it with Chowder? You can't leave the bed, and you can't be sure Chowder will track this thing anyway."

Gran looked down at her hands. She had them clasped together. She started massaging them. She did that when she wasn't happy. "You'll need to hide yourself and stay here. I'll be the bait, and you'll be the tracker."

Mary didn't know how to react. Gran wanted her to track this thing, but she didn't know what to do. This seemed extremely dangerous. Yesterday, Gran had her swearing to not even come to the hospital again until she'd handled the monster. She'd been happy to swear not to. The moment she'd seen that thing, she'd known she was out of her depth, but Gran was now asking her to follow it. Obviously, Gran couldn't, and who did that leave? She didn't want to do it, but she couldn't say no.

Mr. White picked up on her hesitancy. "Helena, this is a lot to ask of her. She's just a kid."

Gran looked at her when she replied. "You can do it. I know you can. All you have to do is follow it. Learn what you can. See if you can find where it rests. You don't have to confront it."

She nodded her head, but she wasn't happy. The door suddenly opened, and Rachel rushed in.

"Mrs. Dubont! Are you all right? I heard you got hurt. Was it the Shadowman?"

Gran smiled at her, and Mr. White snorted.

"You ditched school," Mary said.

"Duh. How was I supposed to stay in class when I didn't know what was going on? As soon as I saw a chance, I left."

"I'm fine, dear. Just a sprained ankle."

"What happened?"

"I slipped."

Mr. White snorted again.

"Rach, I need you to take me to my house to get a few things for Gran."

"Sure, wanna go now?"

"Yeah." She didn't look back as she left. She felt jittery, like she was over-caffeinated. She let Rachel lead the way.

She kept her head down in the elevator. She didn't want to talk to the elevator ghost. She didn't want to talk to anybody. She realized she was scared. She'd just spent the last hour worried that the Shadowman had hurt Gran, and even though it had turned out it hadn't, they were going to stay in the hospital and give it another chance.

When they finally got into the car, Rachel asked, "So what really happened?"

"Gran sprained her ankle on purpose. She requested to be put in Mr. White's room so she could interrogate him."

"Oh my God, your Gran is such a bad-ass."

"Yeah, I guess."

"Has he told you anything?"

"He doesn't know how to get rid of the Shadowman."

"What? After making all those demands, he doesn't know anything?"

"He says they usually don't kill people. They just drain people for a while and then move on."

"What?"

She shrugged her shoulders. "That's what he said."

"Drains them of what?"

"I don't know. He doesn't know what they are, either."

"Well isn't he a fountain of ignorance. Does Gran have any ideas?"

"Not yet," she lied. She didn't want to tell Rachel about the stakeout because she'd insist on being a part of it, and Mary didn't want to put her in danger, too. Never mind herself, Gran, and Mr. White.

She left Rachel in the living room as she went to pack the overnight bag for Gran. She put Chowder's body into the bag first and packed the flashlights around him. She also threw in a few of Gran's Martin and Lewis DVDs in case they needed to threaten Mr. White some more. She barely had room for the normal stuff.

"Hey, Mary, how much longer?"

She struggled with the zipper and finally got it closed. Chowder gave a muffled whine. "Well, if you don't like it in there, come out," she said. She didn't understand him sometimes. He would go into his body and expect them to pet him. She would refuse, but Gran would often sit on the couch with him tucked beside her and pet his sawdust-filled head. It was creepy. She carried the overnight bag downstairs.

"Ready?" Rachel said when she saw her.

She hitched the bag higher onto her shoulder. "Yeah, let's go."

As they went back to the hospital, Mary felt resignation set in. She was going to stay behind in the hospital and wait for the Shadowman to attack Gran. It seemed like such a bad plan, but what other choice did she have? She glanced at Rachel and wished she could talk to her-- because she wanted to talk to someone about how crazy this was--but kept quiet. Rachel didn't notice her uneasiness. She kept both eyes firmly on the road. She was a very careful driver. She had to be. If she so much as scratched the paint, her dad would revoke her driving privi- leges, and he inspected the car every time she came home.

Mary realized she had another problem. How was she going to explain to Rachel that she didn't need a ride home? She couldn't drive her- self, even if she'd had a car. She only had a learner's permit, and no one else was around to take her. Saying she'd take a cab or the bus wouldn't go over.

When they got back to the hospital room, Gran and Mr. White had their dinners before them. Mr. White was poking the food on his tray warily. "I don't suppose you brought some cheeseburgers and fries with you?" he asked.

"Those cheeseburgers and fries are what landed you here in the first place," Gran said, but she was only pecking at her food too. It looked like it was supposed to be beef Stroga- noff, except it was rather gray and mushy.

"Do you want me to go down to the cafeteria and get you something else?" Mary asked.

Gran shook her head and pushed the tray away. "No, I'm just not hungry. Rachel, thank you for driving Mary. Your mother is looking for you. I'm afraid I mentioned you were by, and she realized you must have skipped class. You should go talk to her. Don't worry about Mary. Neil, an old friend of ours, is coming to see me and can drive her home."

Rachel looked reluctant to leave, but Gran had spoken. She turned to Mary and gave her a hug. "Call me tomorrow," she said.

"Will do," she answered, though she dreaded that future conversation. How many lies would she need to come up with the next time they talked? All the lying was making her feel queasy, but her friend didn't notice. She wished she would. Rachel gave them a wave before slipping out of the room.

"Now, bring me Chowder," Gran said.

"You told Mrs. Pillar about Rachel on purpose, didn't you?" Mary said as she brought the stuffed dog over to her.

"Did you tell her about our plan?"

"No."

"She needed to go. It was the easiest way."

"What do we do now?"

"We wait."

"This isn't going to work," Mr. White said.

Gran rolled her eyes. "Don't worry, we'll let you keep a night light on."

CHAPTER 8

Waiting in the Dark

Mary wiggled her toes and massaged her calves to wake them up. She wanted to get up and walk around, but that would've ruined the stakeout. She'd been hiding in the cramped closet for over three hours now. Through slats in the folding door, she could watch the room. Gran and Mr. White were asleep or pretending to be. The room was dark except for a light over Mr. White's bed. He still refused to participate in the trap. She couldn't fault him for saying no to the idea. She didn't like this plan much either.

Gran was in complete darkness on the far side of the room. Mary couldn't tell if she was asleep. She had to have her eyes closed to fool the Shadowman, but Mary was watching for it. When the thing showed up, she was to hit it with the large flashlight. Hopefully the flashlight would be enough to send it away. Turning on the room lights might attract the staff. When the Shadowman fled, she'd set Chowder after it and follow him to wherever he led. The more she thought about it, the less she liked the plan. It all hinged on too many unknowns. What if the Shadowman didn't show? What if the flashlight didn't scare it off? What if Chowder wouldn't follow it? What if she couldn't follow them? It was a little after midnight. The night nurse had just done a check. Mary had been startled to see that it was Mrs. Pillar. She'd have to be extra careful to avoid her.

She'd gone into the closet around nine o'clock when visiting hours ended. Gran and Mr. White had kept the television on for the first couple of hours, and Gran kindly put it on Animal Planet for her instead of the History Channel like Mr. White kept grumping for.

Since the television had been turned off and they'd settled in to sleep, Mary had been sitting quietly in the closet for over an hour. She was bored and getting a little sleepy. She had a cup of coffee with her, but it had long gone cold. The coffee was from the hospitality cart that Mabel had brought around. She'd looked askance at the room Gran had been put in. Mary had heard her mutter something about the cure being worse than the disease.

She cradled Chowder's body in her lap while the ghost dog slept inside it. She hadn't known ghosts slept, but she was getting an earful now of soft snoring sounds. She thought maybe ghosts even dreamed. Chowder would occasionally make little snuffling noises. She didn't know if all ghosts retreated to their anchors to sleep or if it was just a quirk of Chowder's. At least she could just shake his body to wake him when the Shadowman appeared.

Listening to the ghost dog's gentle snoring was really weighing her eyelids down. She took a sip of the cold coffee with a grimace. If she fell asleep and the Shadowman did appear, it could hurt Gran. She wasn't going to let that happen, but she wouldn't let herself hope that it would show up either. She'd be very happy to spend a long, sleepless night in the closet bored out of her mind. She tried to review what she knew about Shadowmen, but it wasn't much. Mr. White had impressed upon her their alienness. They weren't human and never had been. Of that he was sure. What they were was a mystery. They fed off humans. What they took from their victims, though, wasn't clear. Victims of Shadowmen grew irritable and sickly. He said that he knew of no reports of them outright killing someone. What was left unasked was: how would they know if a Shadowman had killed someone? Mary wondered how Vicky was doing. She hoped someone was with her. She also wondered about the patient they had saved. She hadn't had a chance to ask anyone if he had family or friends. If he was alone, he was in danger.

She couldn't worry about the unknown patient right then. She couldn't do anything to help him. She had to watch out for Gran, who, she was pretty sure, had fallen asleep by now. Gran had a flashlight, too--a small one tucked into bed with her--but if she were asleep when the Shadowman came, she might not wake up to use it. She might not wake up at all. Mary pushed that thought away. Gran knew what she was doing. Everything might seem up to chance, but she often had things all figured out.

She let out a long, silent sigh. The waiting was killing her. She settled back into the closet and tried to relax. She wished she had something to do. Chowder continued to gently snore.

It was dark. Too dark. Mary jerked and realized her eyes had been closed for more than a blink. She'd dozed off. Heart pounding, she looked through the slats of the closet. Everything looked the same. She was about to push the folding doors open to check Gran when there was a soft chittering sound. She froze and listened harder.

The chittering sounded like insects or electronics. It was hard to decide which one. It made her ears feel itchy. Her eyes scanned the room back and forth, but she couldn't see any change.

The chittering grew louder. She gave Chowder a little shake. He snuffled a bit.

She caught her breath when a dark form rose up between the beds. It shied away from Mr. White's bed and leaned over Gran's. "Chowder, wake up!" she hissed. Goosebumps erupted up her arms as what she could only describe metaphorically as a shiver dropped from the stuffed dog. A low growl sounded at her feet. Chowder was awake.

The Shadowman was rising over Gran's bed. Mary cradled Chowder's body as she hefted the flashlight. She could do this. She grabbed the edge of the closet door and wrenched it open. She clicked on the flashlight and aimed it at the Shadowman. The light showed wispy tendrils like steam rising from Gran. The Shadowman jerked when the flashlight beam hit it. Its red eyes met hers.

"Get away from her!" she harshly whispered, feeling stupid for having to keep quiet and afraid someone would hear her.

Chowder began barking loud and harshly, like dogs do when they know something threatening was in their territory. She'd never heard him bark like that. He sounded twice his size. It was a good thing only she could hear him.

The Shadowman swooped up the wall and across the ceiling. She flinched and almost fell back into the closet. Her beam shot wildly around the room as she tried to keep up with it, but it was moving too fast.

She felt panic start to creep up on her. They'd expected the Shadowman to flee instantly, like before, but it was only dodging her and going around the room. It swooped from ceiling to walls. It was coming closer and closer, but she had trouble keeping up with its erratic movements. Its weird chittering was getting louder and deeper. It was setting her teeth on edge. She had the suspicion it was trying to get behind her. She didn't want that. Neither Gran nor Mr. White had stirred.

"Gran!" she cried hoarsely. Maybe if they hit it with two flashlights, it would finally go. Chowder was still snarling and barking. His small, vicious presence was comforting, but she didn't know if the ghost dog could touch the Shadowman, let alone bite him.

"Gran!" She took a chance and flashed the light across her face, hoping it might rouse her. She was afraid to move from the closet's entrance. The Shadowman moved too quickly.

Mr. White roused with a snuffle. "What's going on?" he said, blearily looking around.

"It's here. Can you wake up Gran?"

The old man stiffened, and his eyes shot to the ceiling where Mary's flashlight beam was streaking back and forth after the Shadowman. "Helena!" he shouted. Mary winced. He was going to draw the nurses.

Gran jerked upright and then winced as her foot shifted in the sling. "Get your flashlight out and zap that thing!" Mr. White ordered. Gran snatched back the covers and whipped the flashlight out. She aimed it at the Shadowman, and two beams of light were now darting around the ceiling. That seemed to do it. The Shadowman slid down the wall.

"He's gone into the duct! Chowder, go get him! Get him!" Gran said sweeping the light toward the grate. The ghost dog ran, and Mary heard the tapping of paws in the vent.

"Well, go after them!" Gran said, pointing with her flashlight at the wall.

Mary froze. "What?"

Mr. White's eyebrows shot up, and his jaw dropped. "Helena, be reasonable!"

"How else are you going to follow them?"

"I thought Chowder would come find me when he tracked the Shadowman to its hiding place."

"And how were you going to get there? If any hospital staff sees you, they'll stop you."

"But, but..." Mary's eyes darted back and forth from Gran to the vent. Go in there? After the Shadowman? Seriously?

"Is it even big enough for her to get through?" Mr. White asked.

"Yes, I looked. She should be able to squeeze in."

Mary went between the beds and crouched down to look at the vent. It was smallish, but she could probably squeeze through. Gran couldn't have, though. When had she been looking at the vents and judging who could fit?

"I need a screwdriver to open it," she said with a sense of relief. She did not want to go in there.

"Oh give me my purse," Gran said. She sounded irritated. Mary shot her a look. Mr. White had said those touched by the Shadowman became irritable. Gran appeared to be proving that fact. Mary retrieved her purse and handed it over. She rummaged inside and pulled out a small screwdriver.

"See if this will work," she said.

Mary took the small screwdriver unhappily. Her eyes met Mr. White's. He was shaking his head. "Helena, what are you doing?"

"Helping Mary track down the Shadowman. What does it look like?" she snapped. Mary ducked down and set to work on the screws. She wasn't sure if Gran was in her right mind or not, but she wasn't willing to question her in her current mood. Mr. White, however, was.

"Because I wonder if you're helping her track this thing or forcing her to."

Gran ignored his comment, though it seemed to have soured her mood more. "Mary, how much longer?"

"I'm almost done." She could faintly hear Chowder still going through the vent. The third screw came out, and she set to work on the last.

"Hurry up. You're taking too long."

The last screw fell out, and she tugged the vent loose. She started to climb in.

"What do you think you're doing?"

She paused, her heart lifting. Maybe Gran hadn't really meant it. Maybe this was all some sort of weird test or lesson, and she'd call off the pursuit and tell Mary that she'd never ask her to do something so dangerous and foolhardy.

"You need to take Chowder's body to let him keep up with the Shadowman and a flashlight to ward off the fiend. Really, Mary, where's your head?"

Her face felt tight as she took the two items and set them in the vent. "Sorry," she mumbled.

"Helena!" Mr. White shouted.

"Will you shut up! You'll draw the nurses. Mary, get a move on."

"I'm moving."

It was with a small sense of relief that she wiggled into the duct and away from Gran. As she set the vent back, she wasn't sure, but she thought she heard Gran say, "Be careful."

The caper movies always made climbing through air ducts seem easy. With upbeat music and a humorous montage, the movie dare-doers would scamper through the ducts with ease. After going ten feet, Mary could sagely say that crawling through air ducts was not fun, that she'd highly recommend knee pads, and she wished there was a montage to speed things along. She didn't like it in there, not one bit.

The vent wasn't very tall. Instead of crawling on her hands and knees like a baby, she was on her stomach, pushing and pulling herself through the duct. There wasn't enough room for her to turn around, either. If the Shadowman stopped and waited for her, there was nothing she could do. The more she thought about the whole situation, the worse it seemed.

She passed vents into other rooms. Most were dark and silent--plenty of places for the Shadowman to hide or feed--but she knew it wasn't in any of the darkened rooms. Chowder was still ahead of her.

Even after seeing the Shadowman feed a couple of times now, she still didn't understand what it did. She figured Gran had been affected by the Shadowman, at least she hoped that's what had made her so snippy and cranky. She'd rarely seen her that way before.

That thought made her pause. Mr. White may claim to never have been attacked by the Shadowman, but how would he know? Gran seemed to accept his attitude as normal, but maybe he'd been a victim, too.

The possibility of Mr. White having been a victim without anyone having noticed reminded her of Kyle. He'd been extremely confrontational with her when they'd first met. When she'd asked him why he'd hated her at first, all he'd been able to stammer out was that Vicky had said some stuff and obviously the cheerleader hadn't liked her, and he'd wanted to get in good with Vicky, so he'd been mean to her. And then he'd been possessed by a homicidal ghost and no one had noticed.

There was a moral in there about being nice and caring, but Mary didn't put much stock in it. If everyone was sickeningly sweet to each other, the world would implode. Anyway, it didn't matter, because even if someone was the vilest form of human being, there were still suckers who would climb into ventilation ducts to help them.

A distant bark broke into her downward spiral of thoughts. Chowder was still out there, and he couldn't be that far ahead of her. He couldn't roam more than ten yards away from his body, which she still carried. She started crawling again and eventually came to a vertical duct. She could not imagine lowering herself into it but peered down anyway to take a look. It was pitch black. She shined the flashlight down. The beam bounced off the aluminum walls without skimming over any shadows.

"Chowder!" she whispered.

There was no answer. She slithered backwards to the nearest vent and pushed on the grill. It was screwed in from the other side like Gran's, but it looked like it opened onto a supply closet. She pushed with her hands as hard as she could, but it didn't budge. She maneuvered herself so her boots were aligned with it and pressed her feet against it and pushed with her legs. With a terrible protesting shriek, the vent popped out from the wall. She scrambled out, scraping herself a few times. The scrapes hurt.

This was such a stupid idea. She should've just snuck down the hallway instead. It wasn't like Gran could've done anything to make her go into the vent. She expected the supply closet door to open and for someone to appear who would escort her out of the hospital. She actually wanted that to happen. She was tired, she needed sleep, and she had no clue what she was doing. Being sent home would be a blessing, but she couldn't give up and just leave. Gran would have her hide. The whole situation sucked.

"*Arf! Arf!*" Great, Chowder was back. At least, the Shadowman hadn't eaten him.

"Where have you been?"

The next bark she heard was from the other side of the supply door. Funny how he didn't seem to expect her to crawl through the ducts. She peeked into the hall. It was empty. Chowder barked again, and she heard his paws tapping toward the stairwell. She followed him down three flights to the basement. At the bottom of the stairwell, there was a metal door with a sign that read "Authorized Personnel Only", but when she tried the handle, it opened. She wasn't sure if that was good or bad luck.

The door led into a narrow passage. It was dimly lit, and the walls here were made of cinder block. Chowder barked from the end of the passage, where it opened up. She walked forward and found herself in a machine room. Pipes snaked up to the ceiling and large air handling units grumbled all around her. It wasn't well lit. There were lots of shadows.

She turned on the flashlight and started aiming it into all the dark corners. "Chowder?"

He began growling and the chittering began again. "Chowder, come here!"

She was supposed to just check out where the Shadowman went and see if she could find out anything else about it, but Chowder seemed to have a different plan. By the sounds of his growls, he'd really like to find out if ghosts could bite Shadowmen.

She crept further into the mechanical room. She wished she could see ghosts, because trying to track Chowder's growls as they reverberated off the metal pipes was not proving easy. She circled round a dark boiler and came to the back corner of the room. She aimed her flashlight into the corner, and red eyes flashed in the beam. She quickly dropped the beam to the floor.

"Chowder, come here."

The ghost dog kept growling.

"Chowder, get in your body. Get in your body now!"

She set the dog's body down on the floor. It was a punishment measure at home. When he became too unruly or hyper, she would send him to cool off in his body. It was the incorporeal version of being sent to the dog house. Chowder whined. "Body," she repeated, pointing at it.

Chowder whined one more time but went into his body. She picked it back up and tucked it under her arm. The chittering died down and was replaced with a purring sound. If she hadn't known it was coming from the Shadowman in the dark corner, she would have confused it with the mechanical sounds.

Without the light shining on it, she couldn't distinguish the Shadowman from the rest of the darkness. All right, what now? She was alone in a room with it. What was her next move? She decided to go with simple. "Hello?"

It didn't respond.

She didn't know if the Shadowman could understand her, but talking was all she had. "You shouldn't be here. You need to go somewhere else. The people here are sick and weak. Feeding off them isn't right. You're doing them a lot of harm." She didn't know where else would be better. The whole feeding off people thing was bad anywhere, but doing it to the sick and weak had to be worse.

"Do you understand me? Do you think you could go somewhere else?"

Still no response. Should she leave? She wanted to pretty badly, but what about Vicky, Gran, and everyone else in the hospital? They couldn't leave.

"You're hurting people here. If you don't go away, we'll have to stop you." Just don't ask her how. "I mean it. People are getting upset, and they'll come after you."

Nothing. The purring sound hadn't changed while she spoke. It hadn't understood a thing she'd said. This was useless. It wasn't human and had never been human; reasoning with it

139

was futile.

Since it seemed content to stay in its dark corner, she panned the flashlight around again. Everything looked normal. There were several large boilers, air-handling units, water heaters, and pipes everywhere. She tried to look for something small that could be an anchor for a Shadowman, if Shadowmen had anchors. They really were flying blind with this whole Shadowman thing. Flying blind in the dark. Nothing could go wrong. Obviously.

Chowder growled in her arms. She turned and stumbled backwards in surprise. The Shadowman had slipped closer to her and had stretched out his dark hand towards her.

"No!" She hit him with the flashlight beam and began backing away.

The Shadowman's hand dropped and it swooped away, but then began zigzagging back toward her like earlier in Gran's and Mr. White's hospital room. The chittering sound started again.

CHAPTER 9

Ignore the Dead

It was near to impossible to keep the flashlight beam on the Shadowman. The beam was too small, and the Shadowman was moving too fast. She decided to make a dash for it, back to the stairwell.

As she ran, she held the flashlight over her shoulder and blindly swept the beam behind her in an attempt to keep the creature back, but the chittering sound kept pace with her. Chowder continued to snarl, but he did so from within his body, tucked safely under her arm.

She reached the stairwell door, but her tug slammed her into it. Locked? She didn't understand how that could've happened. This was definitely bad luck, and she decided that the door being unlocked earlier had been bad luck as well. She should never have gone in. Next time she'd obey the official signs--if there was a next time. She pulled as hard as she could. The door didn't even rattle. She turned back. The

Shadowman was lurking at the mouth of the passage. The weak fluorescent lights began to flicker, and the darkness between each flicker lengthened.

She jumped when a shiver skimmed her leg. Chowder had dropped from his body. "Chowder, get back here!"

The little dog barked sharply, and the Shadowman hissed. She saw its red eyes go to a point on the floor between them. So it could see ghosts. She wasn't sure if that meant anything, but at least she knew where Chowder was. The Shadowman turned around and began making a grinding sound that must have been its version of a growl. It was focused on Chowder and obviously did not like the ghost dog. She crept back down the passage. Chowder continued barking at the other end of the hall. When she was about six feet from the Shadowman's back, she aimed the flashlight and hit the power button. The beam hit it square in the back. As it hissed and swooped out of the way, Chowder's barks receded into the mechanical room. She rushed to the end of the passage and peered around the machinery. Where had they gone?

A flash of light caught her eye. She turned and saw the edge of a swinging door as it shut. Chowder barked again. He'd found a way out for her! Scanning the room for the Shadowman, she ran to the hidden door.

Out of the corner of her eye, she saw something swoop at her. As she pivoted to avoid it, she lost her balance and fell to the chilly cement floor. Tears sprang to her eyes as her backside hit cement, but she held onto the flashlight and waved it around. The Shadowman swooped back into the ceiling shadows. She scrambled to her feet and swept the flashlight blindly all around her. She pushed through the swinging doors and ran down another corridor. Dim fluorescent lights ran along the center of the ceiling. Another set of swinging door flapped at the other end.

She dashed through the second set of doors and was relieved to find herself in a better lit passage, but she didn't know where she was or how to get out. "Chowder?" she whispered.

She heard a ding. She went down the corridor and peeked around the corner. A couple of orderlies had exited an elevator. They began coming her way.

She moved back and looked for a place to hide. She still didn't want to be caught. Chowder barked again, and a swinging door flapped. She quickly slipped into the room and immediately crumbled to the floor, clutching her head.

"I was only going to get a jug of milk." "Hope Ron finds someone else." "Probably shouldn't have

*done that." "About time." "Hello?" "What hap-
pened?" "Wait, I think I made a mistake." "Bitch
stuck me!"*

She didn't need to look over her shoulder to
know where she was, but she still looked. Two
rows of gurneys lined the walls and each one
held a body with a toe tag. She moved to bolt
back outside, but a sharp tug on her pants leg
kept her in place. Chowder was keeping his wits
about him. She, on the other hand, felt like hers
were dribbling out her ears. She was vaguely
aware of the orderlies walking by, but all of the
other voices drowned out their muted conversation.

*"Mom always said to look both ways. Can't be-
lieve something like this got me." "He's not good
alone. His apartment was a pig sty before I moved in,
but he began picking up after himself when I started
living there." "But it was SO awesome. I mean like
Guinness Book awesome." "Can't believe they
dragged it out so long." "Are you all right?" "Where
am I?" "I told the shrink that the meds weren't working." "Gonna get her for this."*

She tried to block them out, but she wasn't
hearing them with her ears. She didn't know
how she heard ghosts. She just did. Now they
were crowding her head, and it hurt.

*"At least I wasn't running with scissors." "Just
needs someone around to tidy up for." "Hope they got*

it on tape. I'll be legendary." "Idiots." "Do you need help?" "I remember going to sleep. Am I dreaming?" "I don't think this made things better." "Nobody hurts me and gets away with it."

She needed to get away before the ghosts figured out she was there. It sounded like one already was aware of her. She clenched her jaw to make sure she didn't respond. If they became aware of her, the situation would get worse. Talking around her hurt, but if they began talking to her, her brain might fry. Too much input or something. She just knew it was bad. Once in a thrift shop, she'd encountered a small glass box full of thimbles. It had sent her to her knees. Luckily, Gran was with her and understood what was happening. She'd hustled her out and given her some aspirin. The box had held a collection of twenty thimbles. Each one had its own ghost. The ghosts had been singing "Row, Row, Row Your Boat" of all things. They'd been doing it in rounds. The overlapping voices, the sound, whatever had sent Mary's brain into a tailspin. She didn't know what had happened to the small glass box, but then again, she'd never gone back into that shop.

This wasn't as many voices, but their various talk was pounding on her head. She carefully looked out the small window in the door and saw the orderlies coming back. She ducked down again and waited for them to go by. They walked back to the elevator, the doors dinged, and then three quarters of the lights turned off. Things had just gotten worse.

The chittering was instantly audible outside the morgue doors. Chowder began barking again. She blindly backed away and jostled a gurney. She jumped and whirled around. She carefully pulled it back into line. She was shaking.

"What's that?" "Who's there?" "What is that thing?" "Whoa." "Is that what you're hiding from?" "Please let this be a dream." "Don't like this." "What the hell?"

Mary tried to think. She had the flashlight and Chowder. She was in a room full of ghosts. They were aware of the Shadowman. She didn't know how she could use that.

The Shadowman began slipping into the room through the crease between the doors. She raised the flashlight and hit it with the beam. It slipped back outside, but it had her cornered. There wasn't any other way out of the room. She was shaking so badly that the flashlight beam jumped wildly all over the door. It was difficult to keep it along the seam. She needed help, but the only help she had was dead. She knew it was a bad idea, but she cleared her throat and said, "I do need help."

"What'd she say?" "Who is she?" "That thing is not cool." "She shouldn't be here." "How can I help?" "Will someone please tell me what's going on!" "I used to cry a lot, too." "Want her to blubber like that."

She clutched her head and doubled over. "Please, I need help! Can someone turn on the lights? That thing will go away if there's light!"

"Is she talking to us?" "Poor girl." "This is like having front row seats at a horror movie." "You should be more careful." "I'll see what I can do." "Am I dead?" "I used to be afraid of the dark too, but I guess it's stupid to be afraid of anything now." "Ha-ha, it's going to get you."

She crumbled to her knees. There was so much pressure on her head. Their words piled on her like rocks.

"One at a time! Can't you speak one at a time! What good is all this chattering over each other?"

"She can hear us?" "She can hear us?" "She can hear us?" "She can hear us?" "She can hear us?" "She can hear us?" "She can hear us?"

Mary whimpered. Chowder barked sharply. She winced and stroked his head. She didn't need him adding to the cacophony as well. She kept an eye on the morgue doors. Her flashlight's beam rested on one of the windows. The Shadowman was still out there. It was making the purring sound again.

"Miss, can you hear us?"

She pulled her eyes away from the doors to look back into the room. Her eyes skittered over the gurneys. She may talk to ghosts all the time, but dealing with evidence of their deaths was not easy for her. She'd been weirded out by Chowder the first time and still was occasionally, but having the bodies--she shuddered when she realized that the correct term was "cadavers"--there before her was quietly horrifying.

"Miss?" It sounded like the one who had been struck by a car was speaking.

"Yeah, I can hear you."

"Do you know what's going to happen to us?"

She shook her head.

"But we're dead?" This was said by the one who seemed to have passed in his sleep. Ironic how people thought that was the most peaceful way to die, because it seemed to be very disorienting for the ones who suffered it.

"Yeah, you're dead. You'll go somewhere. I know that much. You aren't stuck here. It may just take a few days. Don't try to stick around. Trust me. It isn't better than what's next."

"How do you know? You just said you don't know where we'll go." This was said by the woman who was worried about her boyfriend or husband.

"I know because I've met other ghosts. None of them have been happy. Most of them ended up twisted and mean."

"Your dog seems happy." This was from the girl who'd committed suicide.

She glanced down at Chowder's furry head. "Yeah, but are you a dog?"

No one replied.

Suddenly, the lights began flickering on. Relief coursed through her as she looked up. There was a screech from the hallway and a crash. She crept to the morgue doors and warily stuck her head out. The hallway was lit, and the doors to the mechanical room flapped.

"It's gone. What was that thing?" This was the one who had helped her.

"It's called a Shadowman. You don't need to worry about it. Thanks for turning on the lights."

"Will you be all right?"

"Yeah, I'm going back to my gran's room. Thanks again."

"Be careful."

"Yeah. Bye."

"Tell my wife I love her." "Tell Ron to remember me by being happy." "Hey, could you check to see if I'm on Youtube?" "Can you make sure they honor my wishes?" "You better hurry." "Are you sure I'm dead?" "Wait, could you tell my parents I'm sorry!"

"Tell my cheating girlfriend to sleep with one eye open."

She didn't have the energy to run, though she wanted to. She kept her head down as she stumbled to the elevator. The voices trailed her, but she didn't acknowledge them. She pressed the call button repeatedly. This was what she'd dreaded. Not only were all of their voices making her head throb, but their requests were impossible. She couldn't impart any last messages or fulfill requests. They were dead, and she had to live her life.

"Tell her I'm sorry." "Ron needs to find someone nice. Make sure he knows he needs to find someone nice." "Ooh, I wonder how many views it's gotten. I bet it's gotten a ton. Read me the comments. I bet they're awesome." "There better not be any funny business over my will. Tell them I wanted it all to go to charity, and they should grow up." "Take care." "I think you're lying. I don't feel dead." "If I had another chance, I wouldn't have taken the pills. Tell them." "Better yet, slap her. Say it's from Miguel."

She practically fell through the elevator doors when they opened. *"Wait, when will you be back?" "Don't go yet." "Hey, you'll need my screen name." "Don't you need my address?" "Get some rest. It looks like you need it." "Wait, come back." "You didn't even get my name!" "Bitch, you're as useless as her."* She pushed the button for two and let out a sigh as the doors closed. Alone in the elevator, she slid down the wall and held Chowder close, relieved by the silence.

She shuffled back to the hospital room, feeling wiped out. Amazingly, no one saw her. All she wanted was to curl up and go to sleep, though she wasn't looking forward to doing that in the closet, but sunrise was still hours away. She let herself into the room. The lights were still on, and Gran and Mr. White were still awake. Mr. White seemed relieved by her return. Gran, on the other hand, looked annoyed.

"Well, what did you find out?"

She dropped into a chair and set Chowder down. "I'm fine, thanks for asking."

"I can see that you're fine. What did you find out?"

She was too tired to argue or get upset. She just wanted to get some shut-eye.

"It went to the basement. It tried to come after me."

"What else?"

She let her head roll back and stared at the ceiling. "He can see ghosts, and ghosts can see him. They don't seem to like each other."

"What else?"

She shrugged.

"What were you doing down there?"

She didn't reply.

Mr. White spoke up. "What did you expect her to find out?"

"How to stop it; if it had an anchor like a ghost; something!"

"Sorry, I couldn't investigate too much, what with the running and the terror."

Feeling that the interrogation was over, Mary lurched from the chair and went to the closet. She crawled inside and curled up on the floor with her pilfered pillow. She could hear Gran and Mr. White talking, but it didn't keep her awake.

~ ~ ~

"You're telling me there's nothing you can do?"

Mary looked around the hospital room groggily. She turned to Vicky and groaned. She just wanted to sleep. Not have weird astral projection, mind meld, telepathic whatevers with Vicky.

"God, you look like crap."

"Good, that's how I feel."

"So you went to the basement, the thing chased you to the morgue, and the only way you escaped was by getting a ghost to turn on the lights for you?"

She nodded and then frowned. She was having trouble keeping track of the dream. It felt like she'd been there a while and had obviously told Vicky what happened, but she couldn't recall it. Could she be too exhausted to dream?

"Mary, stay with me. The solution seems pretty obvious."

She scrubbed her face in an attempt to wake herself up and then got confused because she was asleep and didn't want to wake up, not yet, at least. She was too tired to keep anything straight. "What?"

"Get a ghost to fight this shadow thing! You said it didn't like Chowder, that it could see it and what not. Well, it sounds to me like it was more than annoyed by it. It wouldn't come into the morgue with all the ghosts in there. I think a ghost could kill it or whatever."

"But it did try to come into the morgue. I held it off with the flashlight."

"Yeah, but it doesn't sound like it tried really hard. I bet it was wary of the ghosts."

Mary shook her head. She wasn't seeing it.

"Get a full-grown ghost, not some little toy dog, sic it on this thing, and you'll see."

"Chowder's a small terrier, not a toy dog."

"Focus!"

"Fine, where am I going to get a ghost?"

"Do I have to think of everything? Figure that out yourself."

"I'll be so happy when you're out of this coma."

"Me too. Now find a ghost, bring it here, and get rid of that thing."

She rolled her eyes at Vicky's bossy tone. "Anything else?"

"Yeah, wake up."

"Oh, come on! Can't I have some normal sleep for a bit? I've been up all night."

"Nope, you need to wake up."

Mary let out a groan as she sat up in the closet. Sleeping on the floor in a small, cramped space had not done her any good. She rubbed her eyes and peered between the slats.

Gran was awake with her breakfast in front of her. "Mary, are you up?"

She opened the closet and got up stiffly. She walked slowly to the chair by the bed and sat down. "Would you like some coffee?" Gran asked as she offered her cup.

She took it and drank it down. "Had another chat with Vicky. She thinks a ghost can handle the Shadowman."

"That the girl in the coma?" Mr. White asked.

She nodded. "It's a possibility," Gran murmured.

"Yeah, but where are we going to get a ghost to help us? I doubt any we meet will want to lend a hand."

"I may know one," Mr. White offered.

They turned to stare at him. "He'll probably love it," he muttered.

Before Mary could ask for more details, a doctor and Mrs. Pillar came in. The doctor checked Gran's ankle and chart. He prescribed some pills and told them she could go home.

"When you're ready, come get me, and I'll give you a ride," Mrs. Pillar offered.

"Why thank you, Laura. I'll send Mary to you within the hour."

The doctor and Mrs. Pillar left. Mary began packing Gran's overnight bag. "Who's this ghost who might help us?" Gran asked.

"A guy by the name of Horace Thistlebottom. I've got his anchor back at my shop."

"Horace Thistlebottom?" Mary couldn't believe the name.

"I think he changed it professionally, but he'll help. He can't resist a damsel in distress. That's a personal quote of his."

"When can we come by to get the anchor?"

"Later today, if you like. I can discharge myself. Give me a call." Mary wondered what exactly Mr. White was in for. She'd never gotten any clue. She had a sinking suspicion it was just to harass the staff.

"Mary, go get Laura. I'm ready to go," Gran

said.

Mary found Mrs. Pillar at the nurse's station. They walked back with a wheelchair and a pair of crutches. Mrs. Pillar instructed Gran on the best use of the crutches and told her to stay off her feet as much as possible. She helped Gran into the wheelchair. Mary gathered all their stuff and followed them out.

As she was leaving, she turned back to Mr. White. "Thanks for helping us."

He nodded his head. "Yeah, I can't believe I'm not charging you two for any of it. Hang in there, kid."

She gave him a smile and hurried to catch up with the two women. The drive back was filled with chitchat as Gran and Mrs. Pillar caught up with each other. She sat in the back seat and kept nodding off.

When they got home, Mrs. Pillar helped her get Gran into the house and onto the sofa. She instructed them again on the meds and let herself out.

Gran lay back on the sofa with a heavy sigh. "I think we both need a nap. Go get some rest, and I'll do the same."

"Yell for me if you need anything. Don't try to get up. If you do, I'll tell Mrs. Pillar."

Gran swatted playfully at her. "Get some rest, Mary. You need it."

She didn't argue. She felt dead on her feet. She climbed the stairs, toed off her shoes, and fell into bed. She just wanted to sleep for a couple of days and not worry about anything. Not Shadowmen. Not Vicky. Not anything.

CHAPTER 10

Soliloquies

Mary walked along the neatly trimmed graves carrying a bouquet of dark purple irises. She brought them every time she came. Gran had told her a long time ago that they were her mother's favorite. Her father didn't have a favorite flower, but Gran had assured her that he would like them just as much as her mom.

There wasn't any special reason for today's trip to the cemetery, at least not one Mary knew. Gran would just sometimes decide that they needed to go by. She figured the Shadowman had somehow prompted this visit, but she couldn't figure out how. She'd thought they would stay home and rest, but Gran had insisted, and Mary couldn't very well say no. Who said no to going to their parents' grave? She couldn't even let herself feel resentful. It was important to remember loved ones, even ones she couldn't remember very well.

Gran would usually drive her out, spend a

few moments with her at the grave tidying it up, and then would leave to wait in the car while she had a private moment. Today Gran couldn't even leave the car. Mary had never made the trip to the grave by herself. It felt very lonely, not just lonely but solitary, like maybe she was the last person on earth.

It might seem strange, but she'd never heard a ghost in the cemetery. She didn't know why exactly--like if it were due to the embalming process or something--but the dead didn't linger here. It was ironic, but also a relief. She couldn't imagine what would happen if every grave had a ghost attached to it.

She finally came to a stop at her parents' grave. The tombstone was a double marker in dark granite. Johanna and Henry Hellick, loving parents both killed May 5th, 2000. She lay down the irises and took a seat.

"Hi, Mom and Dad. It's me, Mary." She knew it was silly to tell them who it was, but it was how she started every conversation with them since she was little. It was like a ritual now.

She paused a moment as she collected her thoughts. They had died when she was four. A drunk driver had crossed the center line and plowed into them. She'd been in a child's car seat in the back when it had happened. She re-membered them in a vague sort of way. She could recall a sense of love and warmth. Everything else that she knew had been gleaned from Gran and photographs. She didn't really know them and never would, but she still felt a connection. They were her parents. That meant even dead, they were a part of her life, a part of who she was.

"I'm a junior now in high school. The year has been pretty good so far, I suppose. Rachel's still my best friend. I'm still making good grades. I got my learner's permit. Gran's been trying to get me to drive, but I don't like it. I'm probably the only teenager in America who isn't eager to get behind the wheel, but there you go. I know I need to learn, but I'm worried that I'll make a mistake or someone else will make a mistake and bam! I'll get over it eventually.

"We got a ghost dog for a pet. His name's Chowder. He's pretty great. Don't tell him or Gran that I said that. His previous owner gave his body to us. She'd taken it to a taxidermist. It's kind of weird having his body. He's a Scottish Terrier. He's pretty cute. Man, I should've brought him to meet you. Anyway, he helped me get rid of a really nasty ghost a month ago. The ghost was haunting the house of a guy from school. The guy and I were friends, but we sort of aren't anymore. He doesn't like any of the paranormal stuff. His brother seems a little cooler about it, which is ironic considering he was possessed." Her eyes drifted off the tombstone as she thought about that whole debacle. She really didn't want to rehash it any further. "Anyway, Mr. Landa is still working on making me a nice, well-adjusted member of society. I don't think he's made much progress.

"Gran just got out of the hospital. It wasn't serious, just a sprained ankle, but she put herself there on purpose, which is insane. She wanted to badger an old man for help because we're trying to stop a Shadowman from hurting patients at the hospital. A girl from school is the one who told me about it, except she's in a coma, and she told me in a dream. So nothing weird there. I've been trying to help her, but it seems pretty hopeless. We don't know what will get rid of the monster."

She hung her head. "This thing scares me pretty bad. I don't know what it is. It isn't a ghost. Mr. White says it wasn't ever human. I believe him. It's an honest-to-God monster."

She picked at the grass as she struggled to push her fear back. It rose up so easily when thinking about that thing. "We think a ghost might be able to stop it. Mr. White has offered the anchor for one that he thinks will help us. He didn't tell us much about the ghost except his name: Horace Thistlebottom. With a name like that, I'm not holding out much hope."

She paused again to think. She really didn't know why Gran had decided that today would be a good day to go to the cemetery. She looked at the tombstone for a few more moments, tracing the letters etched into it with her eyes. "I wish I were normal. I wish I had a normal life. Like I could sit here and tell you about a new dress, or a party, or something nice, and not about ghosts and Shadowmen. I try to stay strong. I really do, but I wish I didn't need to." She looked up at the sky and tracked clouds for a few moments. She turned back to the grave with wet eyes. "You'd probably say I'm doing good and that you're proud of me, but I wish I were normal, and life were ordinary, and you were alive to tell me everything was going to be okay." She rubbed her eyes and stood up. "Sorry for getting weepy. I know it doesn't do much good. See you next time."

When she slipped into the car, Gran looked at her silently. Mary gave her a small smile but couldn't think of anything to say. Gran didn't seem to expect anything. She just reached across and patted her arm. "Let's go to Ezekiel's," she said. Mary nodded and started the car. With Gran's sprained ankle, she couldn't drive, which left Mary to chauffeur. This was the biggest bit of fallout from the hospital incident. She checked her mirrors carefully, turned on her blinker (even though they were on an empty lane in the cemetery) and put the car in drive. Actually, driving in the cemetery was the best place for her. She drove everywhere like she was in a funeral procession. Gran said she just needed more practice, but after losing three hubcaps so far, Mary was beginning to wonder.

"You'll take a right out," Gran offered.

She nodded and carefully steered down the lane. She was holding the wheel too tightly and watching the road too closely, but she couldn't help it. She was in a machine of death. She couldn't help being overly vigilant. She slowly rolled to a stop and checked the street several times. She pulled out and stayed five miles under the speed limit.

Mr. White lived on a narrow side street above his former shop, White's Rare Books. Mary parked on the street, only scraping the tires along the curb and not going up on it, which was an improvement for her. She helped Gran out of the car.

The windows for the shop were boarded up and a cardboard sign was stuck up that said, "Closed Indefinitely." A handwritten note was tacked up under it: "Good Riddance". It seemed Mr. White made as many friends outside the hospital as he did in.

They went to a side door and pressed the buzzer. A screech of "No solicitors!" came out of the box. Gran rolled her eyes and pressed the call button. "Zeke, let us in."

There was a buzz, and Mary held the door. She looked up the staircase that greeted them and glanced nervously at Gran. She'd never manage the stairs with her crutches. Mr. White appeared at the top. "There's a remote down there. Do you see it? Hit the button to call the chair."

Mary picked up the small single button remote and pressed it, not really sure what she was doing. In response to the remote, a chair started descending the stairs on a rail. She had never seen anything like it before. It seemed pretty neat. When it arrived, she took the crutches, and Gran sat down on the chair. Gran took hold of the joystick and started gliding up the stairs. Mary walked a step behind as she followed her up. She sort of wished she could give it a try.

Mr. White was waiting for them at the top. "Any developments since the last time I saw you?"

"It's been only eight hours," Mary commented, as she helped Gran get back on her crutches.

"A lot can happen in eight hours. I found the

sword. This way."

"Sword?" She glanced at Gran. What was she going to do with a sword?

"Come on." Mr. White was already moving. The landing was cluttered with stacks of old newspapers and junk mail. Mary had to pick up piles to make way for Gran.

When they got to the room Mr. White had disappeared into, Mary stopped to survey it. There was no way Gran was going beyond the doorway. The room was filled with overflowing bookcases and jammed with furniture. Newspapers, magazines, and other papers filled this room, too.

"Helena can sit there." He motioned at a chair by the doorway. It had a stack of folders on it. Mary picked up the stack and turned around to find someplace to put it. She ended up putting it on top of another stack that immediately began to spill. She grabbed steadied it quickly, but a good hard sigh would send it toppling.

"Just leave it, Mary," Gran murmured. She carefully sat down in the cleared chair. There was just enough room for her. She had to hold onto the crutches though as there was nowhere to place them. Mary carefully turned away from the precarious stack. At least nothing appeared to be about to fall directly on Gran. Mr. White motioned for Mary to follow him further into the room. They snaked between old beaten-up furniture and had to step over crumpled papers and dirty dishes. Mr. White was in serious need of a housekeeper, or maybe just a keeper.

"Well, here it is." Off one of the bookcase shelves, he picked up a plastic costume sword, complete with plastic, bejeweled sheath. Mary began to think she was being had.

"This is the anchor?"

"Yes. Horace, this is Mary, the young woman I was telling you about."

She waited a moment for Horace to respond. Nothing happened.

"Well, what's he saying?" Mr. White asked.

"Nothing. Are you sure it's haunted?"

"Am I sure? Of course, I'm sure. Horace just plays dumb sometimes. He's chatty enough with me and my spirit board." He shook the sword. It rattled in its sheath. A paste gem fell off. Mary wondered if she should point it out. "Wake up, Thistlebottom. We've got visitors."

He looked to Mary to see if the ghost had responded. She shook her head. From the other side of the room, Gran spoke up. "Maybe if Mary took the anchor, he'll speak. She's a natural amplifier for spirits."

He thrust the sword at her. It looked like something a kid would carry at Halloween. It felt curious in her hands, though. Like Ricky's locket.

She pulled the sword out of its sheath to reveal the gray plastic blade. A cold gust of air swirled around her, raising goose bumps along her arms.

"Blast him, he is always forgetting to unsheathe me. Sometimes, I think it's intentional. No one could be that absent minded and still be able to dress themselves. How do you do, my dear? I understand that you need a champion?"

"Oh, I knew I'd forgotten something," Mr. White muttered as he took a seat.

"Horace Thistlebottom?" she asked.

"At your service, my dear, but please call me Maximilian, or Max, if you prefer. Though Juliet would argue that the name means nothing, I cringe at the sound of my birth name and shudder at the thought of it at the top of a playbill."

"Okay, Max. Has Mr. White explained exactly what we need you for?"

"Maybe you could do so again with more matter and less art?"

She wasn't sure exactly what he meant but figured that had been a yes. "Um, okay, there's this thing called a Shadowman. It feeds off people in the dark. It's been feeding off people at the hospital, which is bad, obviously. We need to get rid it. We know light hurts it, and it doesn't like ghosts. We're hoping that you might be able to help us get rid of it."

"Fear not, I be no Falstaff. I will imitate the action of the tiger; Stiffen the sinews, summon up the blood; Disguise fair nature with hard-favour'd rage; Then lend the eye a terrible aspect; Let it pry through the—"

Mary cut him off. She feared how long he'd go on if she didn't. "I get it. You're willing and able. Thanks."

"Getting stuffy, ain't he?" Mr. White asked. "Imagine if you had to use a spirit board. Takes fifteen minutes to spell out essentially 'Yes, that's right'."

"Humph, unlike some, I choose my words to flow trippingly off the tongue."

Pushing forward, she asked, "What now?"

"Now, we go to the hospital and deal with the Shadowman," Gran said from across the room.

"What, just like that? You don't even know if this will work," Mr. White said. Mary let out a small sigh of relief. Glad someone was erring on the side of caution.

"And how will we know if it will? You have a test Shadowman to try this on?"

"Why am I the one worrying about your granddaughter's safety? Shouldn't you be?"

Gran's eyes slanted to her and then skittered away. Mary wasn't sure what her look meant.

"Mary set out to help her school friend, and the Shadowman is what she found." She stopped herself from correcting Gran's continuing misconception of Vicky.

"Yes, I know that, but why must she be the one put in harm's way?"

"It's just the way it is," Gran muttered and wouldn't look at them.

"Gran?" She understood less now than when Max was talking.

"Helena, explain yourself. It's clear Mary is scared of this thing and doesn't want to face it, which means she has some sense about her, but you're pushing her along like some sacrificial lamb, and she looks up to you too much to speak up. Well, I'm speaking up for her, and I won't let you out of this house with Horace until I get an answer."

A steely glint came into Gran's eyes, but Mr. White's glare was just as flinty. Mary didn't know if she should speak up and, if she did, what she should say.

"Tell me, were these two ever involved?"

Mary jumped and looked down at the costume sword. "What?"

"What is it, Mary?"

"It seems possible to me. They certainly fight like they loved each other once."

"Mary, you don't have to face the Shadowman. If you don't want to, just say so," Mr. White said.

"But who will get rid of it if I don't?" Mary was happy not to have to respond to Max's weird suggestion. Gran did not have ex-boyfriends.

"Exactly," Gran said.

"Exactly, nothing. Someone else can deal with this. You can go on about your life."

Gran didn't answer, just stared at Mary. It seemed Mary would have to be the one to argue this with Mr. White. "Who else can deal with it? You said no one really knows how to get rid of these things, but we at least have a plan. We should try. We're the only hope for those people in the hospital, of which you were one just this morning."

He shook his head. "This isn't your burden."

"Then whose is it? If not me, who? Just give me a name, and I'll leave it to them."

Mr. White didn't reply.

"She will do this with or without your help, Zeke. Accept it. Now, Mr. Thistlebottom, would you be willing to come with us and assist?"

"Quite, my dear madam. It would be an honor." Mary nodded her head to indicate his answer. Gran stood with her crutches.

"We could use your help too, Zeke, but we will be doing this with or without you."

Mr. White threw his arms up and turned away from them. Mary felt bad that he was upset. She appreciated his concern for her. "I know you're just trying to look out for me, but if something isn't done, people will die. There's a possibility that some already have. We have to do everything we can."

He looked over his shoulder at her. "But what if something happens to you?"

She really didn't know what to say to that.

CHAPTER 11

Rude Awakening

She was sitting on a bench at the park. There were kids playing on the jungle gym. She didn't know where Rachel was, but she wasn't worried. She'd be along eventually. It was nice just watching the kids. "I don't know how you did it, but thanks."

She turned to find Vicky, who had just appeared beside her on the bench--or had she been there the whole time? Mary shook her head. "What?" Was she dreaming? Why weren't they in the hospital room?

"The monster's gone. How'd you kill it?"

"You're out of your coma?"

"Not yet. So how'd you do it?"

"Why aren't we in your hospital room?"

Vicky shrugged. "Don't know. This seemed nicer. So what'd you do?"

Mary looked towards the kids. She didn't

feel like she was dreaming, but she decided to go along with it for now. "We haven't done anything yet. How do you know the Shadowman's gone?"

"Don't feel it lurking around anymore. So if you didn't do anything, who did?"

Mary rubbed her forehead. Was the Shadowman really gone? Was she really dreaming of Vicky in the park? Was this really Vicky or was she dreaming a fake Vicky? Her head hurt, and she didn't feel well.

"No one has done anything."

Vicky huffed and crossed her arms. "Then what happened?"

She stared across the park. The kids were playing tag. One was chasing all the others. He was dressed in black. "Maybe it moved on."

"So it's still out there hurting people?"

She opened her mouth to respond, but a tugging at her pant leg made her look down. Nothing was there. She shook her foot to get rid of the sensation.

"How'd we end up at the park? We were always in your hospital room before."

"I said I don't know. You're the freak, not me."

Mary hoped that this was really Vicky and not a dreamed-up version, because dreaming up a Vicky to insult her would mean her subconscious was just evil.

"Pot, meet kettle, Vicky. You're the one who pulled me into your dreams."

"No, I didn't."

Everything seemed to go darker and sharper. The kid, the one chasing the others, had caught a little girl. When he tagged her, she went down and didn't get back up. "You are so the one doing this. Stop denying it." The tugging on her pant leg began again.

"No, I'm not. This is all you. You're the weird one. I'm completely normal. I'm a cheerleader, for Pete's sake." The kid in black was chasing the other kids again. The little girl, who'd been tagged, lay motionless on the ground. Mary wondered if she should get up and check on her.

Wind began whipping their hair. "I'm not doing this. I don't know how."

"Are you sure? You can talk to ghosts. Why not pull me into your dreams?"

The kid in black had tagged another kid, and he went down, too. She looked for the little girl, but she was gone. Something was still tugging at her leg. "I didn't pull you in; you pulled me." She kicked her foot straight out to get rid of the tugging.

"Nuh uh, and why's everything going scary-movie ominous?"

The last boy who'd been tagged wasn't getting up either. She'd never seen anyone play tag like this. She didn't like it. "I don't know, maybe because you're pissing me off?"

"Aha! So you admit it. You're the one causing this."

Mary stood up and turned away from the children. She didn't like watching them anymore. "Talking to ghosts does not mean that I have telepathic dreams. Being able to do one does not mean that I can do the other."

Vicky jumped up, too. "Just admit it! You're a complete freak who does all sorts of freakish things in freaky ways!"

She shook her head and instantly regretted it. She was feeling really sick. "I've never entered anyone's dreams before. Why should I be able to all of a sudden?"

Vicky threw her hands up. "How should I know? I'm in a coma!"

"That's right, you're in a coma. I'm not the one who needed help with no way to ask for it. You did this. You somehow tapped into my head or pulled me into yours so you could tell me about the Shadowman. We shared the first dream before I even knew you were hurt, so you have to be the one doing this. If I could do this, which I can't, why would I have a telepathic dream with you before I even knew anything was wrong? Welcome to Club Freak, Hickey. Here's your membership card."

Vicky's face screwed up as if she were about to yell at her, but instead, something bit Mary's foot hard. She grabbed her injured foot and started hopping around on one leg. She shot Vicky a glare. "Ow! Stop that!"

"Stop what! Why are you jumping around?"

"You bit me!"

Vicky opened her mouth to deny it, but all that came out was barking. Despite her anger and queasiness, Mary couldn't help laughing. Vicky's face turned red. The scene began to waver. Vicky's mouth moved as if she were yelling at her, but all that came out was louder barking. It suited her.

Mary woke up chuckling. The barking was still going on. "Chowder!" She sat up to throw something at him and felt the strangest and most awful sensation as she came up off the bed. It was like she passed through a blanket of static electricity and motor oil. She jerked back and fell off the bed. She looked up and stared into two red glowing eyes suspended in a black nebulous form. A dark translucent hand reached out to her.

"Oh my God!" She tried to scramble away, but her back hit the wall. She reached for her lamp, but realized that it was on the other side of the bed. She gathered her legs to dart around the Shadowman to the door, but it moved in closer to block her escape. Chowder continued to bark his head off.

Her bedroom door opened, and Gran stood there, leaning on one crutch. "What in the world is going—" her voice cut off when she saw the Shadowman. Her hand slapped the light switch by the door, and the ceiling light came on, illuminating the room. The Shadowman hissed and flew to the window. It was open a couple of inches. Mary hadn't opened it.

Gran lurched into the room. "Mary, are you all right?"

Mary pulled herself onto the bed. She felt awful--like she needed a molten hot shower for her soul. "No, I'm not all right. That thing touched me. Oh man, it was terrible." A cold sheen of sweat covered her body, and she felt oily, not physically but psychically. Gran laboriously lowered herself beside Mary.

"Vicky was just asking me about the Shadowman," Mary told her.

"You were dreaming about her?"

She nodded and turned toward the window. Gran turned, too and saw it was open. She lurched over to close it and turned the lock. She stayed at the window looking outside into the quiet night.

Mary got up and looked over Gran's shoulder through the dark window. "Where do you think it went?"

"I don't know, dear."

Gran's voice sounded odd. Watery. Mary put an arm around her. "Gran, you okay?"

She nodded her head, but didn't turn around. "I'm fine. How do you feel?"

She looked down at herself. There was no physical evidence of her contact with the Shadowman, and she didn't feel ill. Maybe she'd woken up before it'd d had a chance to feed. "Okay, I guess. Not even that cranky."

"You should go back to sleep."

"Gran, what's wrong?" Chowder whined. He could tell Gran was upset, too.

Her shoulders sagged. "I'm just tired."

"No, that's not it. You've been acting weird since this began."

Gran turned and moved to the door, but Mary pulled on her arm to stop her. "Gran, talk to me."

She turned to look at Mary, and her face looked so sad. Had the attack upset her that much? "I'm okay, I promise. That thing gave me the wiggins, but that's all."

"That's good." But Gran's voice betrayed the lie. Nothing was good for her.

"Gran, I'm fine. We'll get the Shadowman. Don't worry." She gave her a hug, hoping it would help.

When Gran pulled away, she wiped her eyes. "I can't help worrying, dear. That thing is awful. The thought of you getting hurt makes me sick."

Mary had to question this statement. It didn't mesh with what she'd said at the hospital or at Mr. White's place. "But you've been gung-ho for me to get rid of the Shadowman. You had me climb into a ventilation shaft to track it and then you got upset when I didn't find out much about it." Gran hadn't even seemed to care how scared she'd been through the whole ordeal, but Mary kept that comment to herself.

Gran shifted uncomfortably on her crutch. Mary instantly pulled her computer chair out and made her sit down. Gran motioned for her to sit on the bed. "First, I should apologize for how I acted at the hospital. I did push you too hard. I shouldn't have forced you to go after it."

"You didn't exactly force me," she said, though she definitely wouldn't have gone in if Gran hadn't insisted.

Gran shook her head. "You're a good girl. You listen to me and do what I ask all the time. I shouldn't have asked you to go after the Shad-owman. When I sent you after it, I wasn't thinking straight. It did do something to me."

"What?" She still didn't understand what the Shadowman did. Did it eat souls? Life force? Happy thoughts? What?

Gran shrugged. "It's hard to say. I was afraid, but also angry. Everything was bad. When I made the plan for you to stay, I'd been confident the Shadowman wouldn't actually get to me, so the fact that it had touched me was upsetting. When you seemed reluctant to go after it, it was like you were okay with it attacking me, like it wasn't a big deal."

"That wasn't it at all!" She couldn't believe Gran had thought that.

"I know, but everything was mixed up. I was so upset. I took it out on you, and I'm sorry. From now on, if I ask you to do something that you really don't want to do, tell me no. You can say no to me. I don't always know best."

"But…" Mary didn't know how to argue with her on this. Gran knew better than her. It was a fact.

"No buts. I mess up too and can make bad choices. Don't think you have to do everything that I tell you."

"So…when you tell me to wash the dishes, I can say no?"

Gran smirked. "If you don't have to wash dishes, I don't have to cook. That'll work out perfectly, don't you think?"

Mary smiled. Gran smiled back.

"Do you remember what you said at Zeke's?"

Not sure what she meant, Mary hedged her answer. "Yeah, what about it?"

"You said that we have to help Vicky because no one else can. Did you ever think you wouldn't or couldn't help her?"

She still wasn't sure what Gran meant. "I didn't know how I could help her, so I had to figure it out."

"But you never thought about not helping her."

"At first, I didn't know if it was for real."

"But once you knew that Vicky really needed your help, you didn't think about not helping her. You even signed up to volunteer at the hospital."

"I guess, but I would've rather it'd been someone else we were helping. Vicky is one of my least favorite people, but she couldn't handle this, and I just figured I had to do something."

Gran nodded and looked at the carpet. "Exactly. You know what's right and will do it, no matter what. I admire that in you, and don't want to ever tell you not to help someone. But that also means you could put yourself in danger and get hurt. I don't want that either. I don't want to stop you, but I don't want you getting hurt. I've been struggling with this since your encounter with Ricky. How can you help others while being safe? All I could come up with is: I have to help you and give you whatever support I can. It's hard, because I still don't want you to get hurt. But I know I can't stop you." She sighed and shook her head. "I pushed all my fears aside at the hospital and in doing so, I pushed you. I told you to do the opposite of what I wanted because I thought that you would do it anyway."

"I wouldn't have climbed into that air duct."

"Maybe not, but you would've followed the Shadowman down to the basement."

Her knee jerk response was to deny it, but she held back and thought harder. She wouldn't have done it again. That was for sure. But that was because hindsight was twenty/twenty. If Gran hadn't arranged for her to hide out in the hospital and follow the Shadowman, she would've figured something else out on her own. She'd taken the volunteering job to do just that. She would've poked around and who knew what trouble she would've gotten into. At least Gran had made sure she'd had a flashlight and Chowder to face the Shadowman. "You're right, but I do want you to worry about me and tell me not to do stupid stuff. I need that." She didn't know how else to say it. She wanted someone to care whether she was safe.

"You're right, and I'll start doing that again, but I don't want you to feel like you can't tell me when you're in trouble or when you're trying to help someone with something dangerous. I'll try to help, but I'm also going to fuss."

"Fuss away. Want to now?"

"Yes, I do. That thing is horrible. I hate that you've had to meet it. I wish you hadn't come across it. I wish I could keep you safe and now this thing has followed us home, and you're not safe. I can't keep you safe."

She didn't know what to tell Gran to reassure her, but she tried anyway. "We'll be okay. We can sleep with the lights on, and Chowder's a good guard dog. We'll know if it's in the house."

Gran nodded and got up again. "Yes, we'll be fine."

When Mary crawled back into bed, she pulled the blankets up to her chin but couldn't get her eyes to close. She looked at the door and wished Gran had stayed or told her to come sleep with her in the living room. There was good reason now to be scared of the dark.

"Would you like me to sing you a lullaby?"

Max startled her, and she looked quickly around the room, though she knew she couldn't see him.

"Gran let you out?"

"Yes, she asked me to guard you while you slept. I'm so sorry I wasn't available before."

"Not your fault. We were the ones that thought it'd be better to keep you sheathed. Sorry." Actually, it had been Mary's idea. Though Max seemed okay, the thought of him wandering around the house had made her feel uncomfortable. Having an invisible guest meant privacy was always in question, but she was okay with him now. Someone watching over her was a comfort. Being alone was the scary option. Max started crooning "Hush Little Baby." He had a nice soft baritone. Her eyelids grew heavy.

~ ~ ~

The next morning Mary woke up to loud arguing that sounded like Gran and Mr. White. For an awful second, she thought she was back in the hospital, but being able to hide under her comforter quickly set her straight. She sat up with a groan and looked blearily around the room. It was morning. Very early morning. What did anyone have to argue about this early except about sleep? "Max, you here?"

"Yes, I hope you slept well."

She shook her head as she got up. "What's

going on?"

"Your grandmother called and told Mr. White about what happened last night. He insisted on coming over."

"What for?"

Max didn't get a chance to answer. From downstairs, Gran called up. "Mary, could you come down, please?"

She took a quick peek at herself in the mirror. Her hair was sticking out every which way. She ran a brush through, so she wouldn't look like a troll doll, but didn't bother changing out of her pajamas. It was eight o'clock on a Sunday morning. That was earlier than she usually got up on weekends, never mind on days when she'd been attacked in the middle of the night by a supernatural monster. She padded down the stairs and found Mr. White and Gran sitting in the living room.

"Morning," she said.

"Good morning, dear. How do you feel?"

"Sleepy. What's going on?"

"The Shadowman touched you last night?" She turned to Mr. White with a yawn.

"Or I touched it. There was touching, anyway. Very unpleasant. Why?"

"It may have harmed you."

"It may have, but Chowder woke me up before it could."

"This the dead dog?"

Chowder's body was sitting on the coffee table. Mr. White picked it up and began examining it. Chowder began growling. Mary went over and took the body. "He doesn't like strangers touching him." She tucked the body under her arm, and Chowder settled down.

"I need to check you to make sure the Shadowman hasn't done any harm."

"What about Gran? Have you checked her?"

Mr. White turned to Gran with a glare. "She won't let me."

"Then why should I? I feel fine. I wasn't even grumpy like Gran afterwards."

"How do you know? You could be psychically maimed right this moment."

"Psychically maimed?" She turned to Gran. "Seriously?"

"Maybe it would be good idea to let him look."

"If I have to be checked, so do you."

"I'm fine."

"So am I."

"Mary," Gran said with a subtle scolding tone in her voice.

"You said last night that I could say no. I'm saying no."

"What are you two worried about? I'm not slicing you open. You just need to sit still and let me do some readings."

"What type of readings?" Mary asked.

"Just let me check your chakras."

"Do you want to test the vision in my third eye, too?"

"The third eye is the chakra called Ajna. So yes, I will be testing it."

Mary crossed her arms and stared at him.

Gran relented. "Fine, you can check me first."

"Gran, we don't have to do this."

"What could it hurt?"

"I swear you two don't know what you're trying to pass up. There were people who used to pay me to do this. They'd come from all around to get me to check them."

"Then why'd they stop?" Mary couldn't help needling Mr. White a little.

"Because of a little thing called retirement."

"What do you need me to do?" Gran asked.

"Be quiet and sit still."

Mr. White got up and went to the side of Gran's chair. He closed his eyes and held his hands out over her head. He waved them slowly in the air over her. Mary didn't know what he was doing, but Gran didn't seem to find it strange. She'd closed her eyes and relaxed into the chair. Mr. White didn't ever touch Gran. He kept his hands several inches above her body as he passed over it. He would pause and hold his hands steady at certain spots--like over her chest and oddly, her knees--but never actually touched her.

Mary watched, not sure what was going on. The whole thing seemed vaguely ridiculous to her, but then again, they'd been supernaturally attacked. It wasn't like they could go to the doctor and get checked out. If there was something wrong with them, Mr. White may be the only one who could help them. Eventually, he straightened with a creak.

"You're fine. No lingering ill effects."

Gran opened her eyes and turned to Mary. Mr. White turned to look at her as well. She still wasn't sure about this, but it didn't look like it would do any harm to let him check her.

"Do you want me to sit down?"

"No, it's better if you're standing. I didn't make Helena stand because of her ankle. Just hold still, and I'll take a reading."

She stood still as Mr. White came over to her. He raised his hands and slowly waved them around her head. His bushy eyebrows were drawn together, and his eyes were shut tight.

"What can you tell?" she asked. She didn't feel anything as he moved his hands around her.

"You're a healthy, young woman with a bit of psychic power," he said. He ran his hands a few inches above her shoulders and arms. He bent at the waist and waved them through the air by her legs. He straightened and looked her in the eye.

"You're fine."

"That's it?"

He shrugged. "What did you expect?"

"I don't know, but you spent more time on Gran's knees than on me."

"She's got bad knees."

"Oh, I do not," Gran protested.

"Well, you will."

Gran shook her head.

Mr. White picked up his hat. He was leaving? She didn't want him to leave. He may claim not to know much of anything about Shadowmen, but he was the closest thing they had to an expert. "So what do we do now?"

He shrugged his shoulders. "If you leave the lights on and stay vigilant, it'll move on and not bother you anymore."

"That's it? Your advice is get a night light?" Mary couldn't believe it. Couldn't he offer something more?

"Yeah, so?"

"So? We need to stop it, not hide under the covers."

"Have I not established the fact that I don't know how to stop it?"

"We can figure something out." She wasn't giving up. She couldn't give up. That thing was still out there and had slipped into her room while she was sleeping. There was no way she was going to let that thing get away with that. She wanted some payback.

"Just let it go. It probably came after you because you poked your nose into its business. Just leave it alone."

"I'm not giving up." She'd figure something out. She didn't know how, but there had to be a way.

Gran sighed. "We'll keep an eye on the hospital at least and sleep with the lights on here. Meanwhile, we'll keep looking for a solution."

Mary nodded. They could do that. She could keep volunteering with the hospitality cart and make sure nothing happened. She hadn't planned on volunteering long term, but she could do it. And Gran could read her Tarot cards and maybe get a clue from them.

"You two are making a big mistake," he muttered.

"We'll be careful, Zeke. Don't worry."

"Oh, I won't," he said, standing and jamming his hat on his head.

"Zeke, don't go yet. We haven't had a chance to really catch up. I'd like to hear what you've been doing with yourself."

He shook his head. "No, I best be getting home."

"May I say, ladies, it was a pleasure meeting you."

The plastic sword was resting on the coffee table. Mary picked it up and held it out to Mr. White. "Thanks for loaning us Max."

"Oh, I think he should stay."

"Stay? But surely--"

"Are you sure?" Mary asked.

"Just in case the Shadowman does come back."

"Having him here would make me feel better," Gran said.

"Is that okay with you, Max?" Mary asked, since he'd seemed ready to go.

"I-I suppose. If you ladies are willing to put up with me for a few more days, I'll be happy to stay. Hopefully my assistance won't be needed."

"I'll let myself out. Helena, call me if there are any new developments."

"Of course, Zeke. Thank you."

Once Mr. White left, Mary sat on the sofa and looked over at Gran. "So, what now?"

She shrugged. "The TV works."

Mary picked up the remote and started flipping through channels.

~ ~ ~

Rachel and Mary had grabbed seats in the art room during TAB. Neither of them took art, but it was where the fringe kids congregated. Goths, garage bands, skaters, and of course, artsy folk safely congregated there away from the Shinies and regular kids. Mary almost felt like she belonged.

"You know, I think we're really dropping the ball here."

"What?"

"With Vicky. She's still in a coma, which I'm not really averse to, but there's still the Shadowman. What type of superheroes are we if we can't save one airhead cheerleader? They do it all the time on TV. What's stopping us?"

Mary gave her a noncommittal shrug. She couldn't tell her about any of the stuff that had happened Friday night, when she'd stayed at the hospital, or Saturday night when the Shadowman had attacked her. She knew Rachel would want to know, but she also knew her friend would be angry for being left out. She'd rather not deal with the fallout. There was enough drama in her life. Except for Mr. White's visit, Sunday had been thankfully uneventful. She and Gran had vegged on the sofa. It hadn't been a productive day, but she felt recharged. Max had hung out. He'd played with Chowder, so the little red ball appeared to fly across the room and bob back on its own. It had been quite hypnotic.

"We're scheduled to volunteer after school. We should stop by Vicky's room to see what's going on and maybe talk to Mr. White some more."

"He's out of the hospital."

"He is?"

"Yeah, he got discharged a little after Gran."

"How is she?"

"Grumpy. She had to cancel most of her appointments for the week because of her ankle."

"Huh. Oh, this should be interesting." Rachel's eyes focused past her.

She turned and found Kyle approaching their table. He did not belong in the art room. His letterman jacket and buzz cut head looked out of place among the piercings and rainbow hair colors. "Hey Mary, how's your grandma?"

"Hi Kyle, she's fine. All she did was sprain her ankle. She's home now."

His eyebrows rose. "How'd she do that?"

"She tripped on some stairs. I was worried for nothing."

He looked at his shoes and didn't say anything immediately. Other students were starting to look at him curiously, and Rachel and Mary were being included in that curiosity. If he didn't leave soon, Mary dreaded what the rumor mill might come up with.

"Is that it, Kyle?" she asked to prod him along.

Rachel gave her a light kick under the table. "Kyle, do you wanna sit down?"

Sitting down would be even more suggestive to the rumor mill. She shot Rach a look. She doubted Kyle would want that type of talk. He was a jock. They dated cheerleaders, though she hadn't seen him with anyone since his early Vicky infatuation, but he was definitely a jock. Jocks dated cheerleaders. They were genetically predisposed to each other. He might be nice to Mary, and Rach might have the misguided idea that he liked her, but that would all change if people started whispering about them. To her amazement, he pulled up a stool and sat down.

"What's really going on with Vicky?"

Rachel opened her mouth, and Mary kicked her this time. But she may have kicked a little too hard, judging by Rachel's yelp. Her friend moved her stool away from her.

Ignoring Rachel's scowl, she asked, "What do you mean?"

Kyle looked at them. She knew her little spot of violence had ruined any chance of lying successfully to him, but she wasn't going to tell him the truth, and she wasn't going to let Rachel, either.

"I know something's up with Vicky, and you two are involved. Suddenly volunteering at the hospital, visiting her mom, something's up."

"Coincidence," she said and didn't elaborate. Keep the lies short, simple, and don't waver--that was how to shut someone out. She felt bad about doing it to Kyle, though.

"And your grandma getting hurt at the hospital?"

"She's old and frail." Kyle's lips thinned at her answer. He'd met Gran. She might be up in age, but she was not frail.

"Fine. You don't have to tell me anything. I just wanted to offer my help, but if you don't want it, I'll just go. See ya. Hope your grandma feels better."

He stood up and strode out of the room. She had to restrain herself from calling him back, because what could he do? How could he help? She didn't like the idea of him being upset, though.

Rachel blew out a puff of air in frustration. "You're never going to get asked to prom at this rate."

"Good. Corsages are stupid."

She shook her head. "Seriously Mary, couldn't you have told him something?"

"Like what? 'Hey Kyle, Vicky's been visiting me in my dreams, and there's a monster attacking her. You wanna help me destroy it? I have no idea how, but it's sure to be a good time, except for the screaming and the death. Those are a bit of a bummer."

"He could handle it. He already suspects anyway. Cy doesn't care."

She knew it was pointless to try and defend Cy. He really didn't want to know about or have any involvement with the paranormal. He'd refused to even allow for the possibility of it. Kyle, on the other hand, hadn't rejected the possibility. He could've stuck his head in the sand and refused to believe that he'd been possessed by a ghost, but instead, he'd accepted it and had thanked them for getting rid of Ricky.

"I just want to keep this thing to as few people as possible. You, Vicky, Gran, and Mr. White are already involved. No need to bring in anyone else."

Rachel shook her head. "You're keeping secrets from a lot of people. I hope you can keep straight who knows what."

Mary tried to chuckle at her comment, but it got caught in her throat. If Rachel only knew what she was keeping from her, she wouldn't like it.

"So, volunteering after school today?"

Mary reluctantly nodded. She didn't have anything better to do.

~ ~ ~

Mary was again pushing the hospitality cart while Rachel knocked on doors. They'd left Vicky's room until last.

"Do you know how many brownie points this is getting me with my mom? If I'd known how much she'd like me doing this, I would've signed up sooner."

"So you're going to keep doing this after all this is over?"

"Yeah, it'll be even better once Vicky's gone. You're going to keep doing it too, right?"

Mary flashed on the morgue and felt a shiver go down her spine. She shook her head. "No, once Vicky's awake, that's it for me. I'm never going to be good with hospitals."

Rachel's glance was full of disappointment. Mary could only shrug her shoulders. Hospitals would never hold any appeal for her. She couldn't see continuing, but if Rachel wanted to do it, that was fine. She would just have to do it without Mary.

They came to Vicky's room. The door was ajar. Rachel tapped on it and pushed it open. Mrs. Nelson was inside. She smiled and waved for them to come in.

"Girls, it's so good to see you."

"How's Vicky?" Rachel asked.

Mary fixed a cup of coffee and brought it to Mrs. Nelson. She looked a little better today. The bags under her eyes weren't as pronounced, and her hair was tidy. Mrs. Nelson took a sip of coffee before speaking. "The doctor says there's improvement. She's responding to noises, and she moved her hands a few times."

"That's great," Rachel said.

Mary stood by quietly and looked at Vicky. She couldn't see any change, but then, she wasn't a doctor.

Rachel continued, "You know, Mrs. Nelson, I was reading an article in a science magazine that said there'd been a study that proved leaving a light on with coma patients really helped with the recovery."

"Really?"

"Yeah, Mary, you read that article, too, didn't you? Didn't it say that?"

Did they need to worry about the Shadow-man anymore? Mr. White seemed confident that it wouldn't return to the hospital or her home. But she may never be able to sleep without a night light again. She had to figure something out, but exactly what remained firmly elusive. She didn't want to be afraid of the dark for the rest of her life. It was a childish fear, like the monster under the bed. She wasn't six years old.

"Mary?"

She jerked out of her reverie. "Yeah, it couldn't hurt."

Rachel gave her a tiny glare. Obviously, she'd expected a more ringing endorsement.

"Well, I'll try that. Like you say, it couldn't hurt," Mrs. Nelson said, though her tone was more placating than accepting.

"It will really help. I promise," Rachel said. Mary worried that Mrs. Nelson would begin to doubt Rachel's mental faculties. Night lights for coma patients. It sounded stupid.

"Well, we should be going. It was good seeing you. I hope Vicky continues to improve," Mary said. She wanted out of that room. It didn't hold anything for her. It was the beginning of all of this, and she wanted to get to the end.

"What's going on? Why are you here, Mary? You need to be catching the Shadowman, dimwit."

Everyone turned to the bed. Vicky's face scrunched up, and her eyelids fluttered open. Her eyes found Mary first, and if her words hadn't clearly indicated she remembered everything from her coma, her eyes said it all. There was a determination to them. A cool regard. It made Mary want to squirm.

"Oh my God, Vicky, my baby!"

Mrs. Nelson flung herself over her daughter

and began sobbing.

"Geez, Mom..." Vicky said in embarrassment, but she put her arms around her and hugged her back. Rachel ducked into the hallway and flagged a nurse to alert the doctors that Vicky was awake. Mary was rooted to the floor. Vicky was awake. It was what she'd been striving for, sort of. Vicky was safe.

A doctor came in and went over to the bed. He gently maneuvered Mrs. Nelson out of the way so he could shine a light into Vicky's eyes and asked her how she felt.

Rachel tugged on Mary's arm for them to go. She numbly turned to the door. "Mary, wait!"

She turned back. Vicky's eyes jumped from her mom to the doctor. It was clear that what she wanted to say wasn't meant for their ears. Dropping her head, Mary went to Vicky's bedside.

Almost choking on her words, she said, "Vicky, I'm so happy you woke up. We've been so worried." And then she bent down and gave her a hug.

She couldn't see the other girl's face, but she hoped she didn't look totally shell-shocked. Mary was at least safely pointed at the wall, so she didn't have to mask her true discomfort with the physical contact. Vicky was as stiff as a board against her. Mary hoped the hug hadn't pushed her into catatonia.

She gave Vicky a harsh squeeze and hissed into her ear. "What?"

"God, do you have to be touching me?" she whispered back.

She rolled her eyes. "What did you want to say to me?"

"Is it really gone?"

That was the one question Mary hadn't wanted Vicky to ask, but she deserved some sort of answer. "It isn't in the hospital anymore. You should be okay, but sleep with a light on just to be safe."

"Where'd it go?"

Mary was happy to cut the hug off there. She let go and straightened. "Don't worry. Everything's okay." She gave Mrs. Nelson a wan smile and hustled from the room, dragging Rachel, who looked a little green, along with her.

"Mary, wait!" Vicky called. She stopped dead in the doorway again. Was she ever getting free? She turned back. Vicky was looking better moment by moment. Color was coming back into her cheeks. "Thanks," she said.

She nodded her head. "See you at school."

"Yeah, see you."

She walked to the elevator without stopping. Time to leave. Nothing more to do here. She pressed the call button for the elevator and gritted her teeth as Rachel sputtered behind her.

"You--you--you hugged the Hickey! I can't believe it, and I saw it! How could you do that? Are you okay? Do you need some disinfectant?"

The elevator doors opened, and Mary came face-to-face with Cy. Kyle was behind him like an afterthought. Cy's lips thinned when he saw her.

She didn't know what to say. Luckily, Rachel did. "Hey guys, guess what!"

CHAPTER 12

Secrets Come Out

"Vicky's awake? When?" Cy's eyes widened and left Mary to look down the hall. His whole body leaned in that direction. Mary took a step back to get out of his way.

"She just woke up. Her mom and a doctor are in there with her," Rachel answered.

"Thanks, see you at school." And with that, Cy brushed past them and went down the hallway. It surprised Mary how his dismissal didn't hurt that much. It was no longer like an ice pick to the heart, more of a glancing punch now. Maybe she was getting over him? Kyle hung back. She turned to him. He had his hands in his pockets, and his eyes on the floor. Another feeling came over her. It wasn't a bad feeling. Kind of warm, in fact.

"Hi Kyle," she said.

He looked up at her and then back at the

floor.

"Hey. So you two just happened to be there when she woke up?"

"Yeah, we had nothing to do with it."

"We didn't?" Rachel asked.

Mary shook her head. "No, Vicky woke up on her own."

"So are you two going to keep volunteering?"

"I probably won't, but Rachel might."

"Oh come on, it'll be fun," Rachel whined.

She shook her head. "The hospital is still not a great place for me. Especially not the basement."

"The basement? What's in the basement?" Rachel asked.

"The morgue."

"You got to go to the morgue? When? Where was I?"

"I took a wrong turn. It was a mistake."

The answer didn't placate Rachel. "Some wrong turn," she muttered.

"If you take the stairs at the end of the hallway all the way down, you might be able to get in through the mechanical room."

Rachel's eyes lit up. "Wanna go try?"

She shuddered and shook her head. "No, I never want to go down there again."

Understanding drifted across her friend's

face. "Right. Well, you wanna hang here while I go try? Please? I promise not to get super mad at you for not telling me all about your trip."

Her mouth quirked into a smile. "Okay."

"But I will expect full details when I get back." Mary nodded. With a quick wave at both of them, Rachel headed to the stairwell. Mary wondered if she shouldn't have told her. What if the Shadowman had come back? Rachel had seemed almost bouncy as she left. There was no way she could call her back. She shook her head and decided that she wouldn't worry. If she didn't come back in thirty minutes, then she'd have a meltdown. Kyle was still standing with her outside the elevators.

"Don't you want to catch up with Cy?"

"No. I'm just his ride. I'm glad Vicky's awake and all, but I didn't really want to come here."

"But you used to like Vicky, right?"

"I thought she was hot, but I'm not really interested in her type anymore."

"What type are you interested in now?" Her voice cracked on "now". She could feel herself turning pink. She couldn't believe she'd asked that question.

"I like girls who know how to do stuff. Who don't care what other people think. Who don't pander to anyone and who know they're special anyway."

Everything sort of slowed down as he repeated her words back to her. She had said that to him when she'd confronted him at school while he was possessed. Having him quote her, when describing the type of girl he liked, gave her goose bumps.

"Oh," she said.

He gave her a sort of shy smile and ducked his head. "So now you know," he said.

"Yeah." She didn't know what else to say. She reached blindly for anything to talk about. "So you remember everything from when Ricky possessed you?" she asked.

"Yep," he said with a heavy sigh.

"I'm sorry, Kyle. I can't imagine how awful or strange that must be."

He nodded his head. She wanted to reach out and comfort him in some way, but she couldn't muster the courage. "I'm also sorry for how I was when you came to talk to me the other day. I was a real jerkface."

"You were?" he asked with a wry grin.

"Yeah, I was," she said sincerely. "I seem to be that way a lot with you."

"I don't think so."

She didn't know what to say to that. He liked her. She'd never run into this situation before. She'd skirted it a bit with Cy, and, oh God, he was Cy's brother. Did she not know how to branch out?

In her panic, she blurted out. "Something was attacking Vicky. Rachel and I were trying to get rid of it."

Kyle's eyes widened. "A ghost?"

"No, not exactly." She winced and looked at him out of the corner of her eye. He might be able to handle ghosts, but what about other weirdness?

"What was it?"

Now she wasn't sure if she should've told him anything. "It's called a Shadowman."

"What'd you do to it?"

Invited it home to terrorize her? Mary didn't know what to say. She felt like she hadn't done anything and didn't know what to do. They were taking stabs in the dark or rather at the dark but not getting anywhere. And she realized with a little start that she'd taken too long to answer. The pieces were clearly falling into place for Kyle.

"The thing's still out there?"

"But it's not threatening Vicky anymore," she was quick to point out.

Kyle, for all his bullishness, was pretty intuitive. "But it's threatening you?"

The quiver of her chin belied the lie she was quick to offer. "No, of course not. It wouldn't think of bothering me or Gran. That'd be like suicidal."

"Mary, are you safe?"

"I'm okay. Really."

He didn't look like he believed her. Rachel reappeared around the corner. She didn't look so bouncy anymore. Mary figured seeing real dead people might have woken her up to how not fun being a coroner would be.

"Come on, Mary. We have to go. Maintenance totally busted me in the mechanical room. They said if I wasn't out in fifteen minutes, security would get me."

"Was this on your way to or from the morgue?" Kyle asked.

"To! I didn't get to see a single toe tag. It's such a bummer."

Mary rolled her eyes. She really didn't understand Rachel's fascination with dead people.

"Mary, if you need help or anything, give me a call, okay? I mean it," Kyle said.

She nodded her head and got on the elevator. "Thanks, Kyle. I will if anything comes up."

"Bye, Kyle. Good seeing you," Rachel said as the doors closed.

"What floor, please?"

Mary snorted to herself.

"What?" Rachel asked.

She shook her head. "We're going to the lobby." The L button lit up.

"What? Oh! Is it the elevator ghost?"

"It's gone."

"Yeah, it's no longer at the hospital."

"Good."

"No, it's not good! It's still out there, and it's going to hurt other people."

"Get rid of it."

"How?!"

The ghost was quiet. God, he was useless. She shook her head and stared at the floor.

"So you, Gran, and Mr. White still don't know how to get rid of the Shadowman?"

"Mr. White thinks we can use a ghost, but I don't know how."

"Chowder?" Rachel sounded worried for the spectral dog.

"No, someone else. He likes to be called Max. Anyway, he's supposed to help get rid of the Shadowman, but no one knows how that's supposed to work. I mean the Shadowman hung out in a hospital that's full of ghosts. If ghosts are so dangerous to it, why stay here?"

"Stayed away."

"What?"

"Stayed away from us. Didn't come near."

"Do you know how a ghost would defeat a Shadowman?"

There was no reply. Mary was seriously beginning to wonder if the ghost was trying to drive her crazy. Maybe it was an evil spirit who enjoyed infuriating people until they saw red.

"What's he saying?" Rachel asked.

Her look must have communicated the lack of communication because Rachel stepped back and looked down.

"I don't know why I bother. I tried to do the right thing. No, I DID the right thing, and I'm getting punished."

"Light hurts it. It flees. If it can't flee, light will kill it."

"How can we keep it from fleeing? It's a shadow. It can slip through vents and cracks."

"No, it can't."

"Yes, it can!"

The ghost didn't argue back, but her mind was already churning over his denial, trying to figure out why he had said that. She flashed on her window. It had been raised a few inches. She'd known the Shadowman had raised it, but why would it have had to raise it? It wasn't air tight. There was a seam, though small. And at the morgue, it was pushing the door open, not slipping through the crack.

"You know, this is as annoying as listening to someone talk on a cell phone."

"He said that the Shadowman can't slip through small cracks, and it can't go through doors. It can be trapped."

"Great, then what?"

"Then turn on the lights."

"So...how do we trap it?"

"We lure it with bait."

"Uh, Mary?"

The elevator doors opened, and she strode off with the beginnings of a plan forming in her head. It was still very hazy, but a plan was coming together. She stopped mid-step, and Rachel ran into her.

"What now?"

She dashed back to the elevator and stopped the doors from closing with her boot. "Thank you. You've helped a lot. And sorry for being so rude to you."

"No worries, miss. It's all part of the job."

She wasn't sure what to make of that but nodded anyway and let the doors close.

"What are you planning?" Rachel asked.

"I don't know yet. Come on, I need to talk to Gran."

Her knee bounced the whole ride home. Now that she had a direction, a way to reach her goal, she was anxious to get it done. She'd been so morose about her prospects before, but now she was driven. The car hadn't come to a complete stop before she jumped out and ran up the steps to the house.

Rachel shouted from the car. "Call me when

211

you have a plan!"

Mary hastily nodded and waved to her before bursting into the house. "Gran!" she shouted.

She hadn't needed to shout. Gran was waiting for her in the living room. Mary let her muscles relax. "Vicky's awake."

Gran perked up at the news. "That's wonderful! How is she?"

She shrugged and dropped into the recliner. "She seemed pretty normal. She said to say thanks."

"Well, that's nice. It's good that she's okay."

"I also think we can defeat the Shadowman."

"And how's that?"

"We set a trap. If we can lure it into a room and shut it in, we can turn on a lot of light and kill it."

"That sounds more like a theory than a plan."

Her shoulders hunched a bit. "I don't have the particulars yet, but it's something to work with. We have to get rid of it."

Gran sighed and nodded. "I'll think about it, maybe come up with a few particulars."

She nodded back. "The room doesn't have to be air tight or anything, and Max can help us."

Gran nodded again but didn't reply. Mary could tell she was thinking, but she looked uneasy, too.

"Night, Gran."

"Good night, dear. Sweet dreams."

Mary went up to her room and closed the door. Lure it, trap it, and kill it. That's what she had to do. She had Max. It obviously knew where she lived, so she could tempt it into the house, but how would she trap it inside if it could open a window to slip in? Max? If she kept him sheathed until the Shadowman was there, she could unsheathe the sword to release him, and he could close and guard the window. But what would happen while Max was covering the window? She had to be able to turn on a lot of lights quickly. The switch to the ceiling light was across the room. Her bedside lamp was too dim to do the job.

She fell asleep with every light burning in her room and a flashlight by her side. Max had told her that he'd keep vigil through the house. Still, she had trouble sleeping. Every hour she would wake up with a start and look around the room.

The next day she shuffled down to the kitchen, following the smell of French toast. Gran turned from the stove to give her a smile.

"Good morning, dear."

Mary mustered a grunt. She poured herself a cup of coffee, but she was too tired to bother with cream or sugar. She slumped into her chair with the coffee sloshing over her hands. She couldn't even muster a hiss as it burned her fingers. Gran set a plate of French toast in front of her. She drank what was left of the coffee first. It didn't rouse her at all. She poured syrup onto her toast and may have nodded off for a few seconds. Syrup was close to overflowing her plate when she set the bottle down. She wasn't even sure what day of the week it was. She clutched a slim hope that it was the weekend. She was way too tired to be allowed out in public.

The fact that Gran was standing at the stove finally registered. "You shouldn't be on your feet," she said.

"I'm doing fine."

Since she didn't have the strength to argue, she shoveled a large forkful of French toast into her mouth instead, then instantly regretted it. She was too tired to eat so much. She propped her head on her fist and dragged her fork through the syrup as she made herself chew. She began dozing off again.

"Mary, I'm keeping you home from school."

She blinked open her eyes and nodded. She spat her half chewed French toast into a napkin. She stood up to go back to bed.

"Aren't you going to finish?"

She weaved on her feet. "Too tired," she mumbled.

"Did you have a nightmare?"

"Never slept long enough to have one. I think I'll try sleeping now. Could you wake me up for lunch?"

Gran nodded and took her plate to the sink. She stumbled back up to her room and collapsed onto her bed. Maybe she could become a hard-core night owl until the Shadowman situation was resolved. She could stay up all night and catch up on her infomercials. She could find out how to get rich without really trying or discover a cleaning product that would change her life. It would be great.

When she woke up with a start, it took her a moment to understand what was wrong. She knew something wasn't right. She blinked and realized that it was dark. She shot out of bed. She rushed across the room to the light switch and turned on the overhead light. The sudden illumination stung her eyes, but her heart started calming down in the light. She looked out her window to find the sky chock-full of stars. She'd slept the entire day. She looked at the clock, and it was just after eight p.m. She went looking for Gran.

She'd expected to find her on the sofa, but the living room was empty. She called out to her.

Silence was her answer. She checked the fridge for a note but didn't find one. This wasn't right. Gran should be here. She still couldn't drive. And she wouldn't have left Mary home alone and asleep in the dark.

The light was flashing on the answering machine. There were three messages. She pressed the play button, hoping to hear Gran's voice giving her a sensible reason for why she wasn't home.

"Helena, this is Zeke. I need you to call me. My number's 555-5651." The message was left at 10:30 a.m. Mary wondered if Gran had gone to see Mr. White, but, if so, why wasn't she home yet?

Next was Rachel. "Mary, where are you, girl? Call me." She waited tensely for the third message, hoping it would be Gran. Instead it was Mr. White again. "Helena, I hope you get this message. I'm worried. Call me."

She picked up the phone and dialed Mr. White's number. It rang three times before he picked up. "Hello? Helena?"

"Mr. White, it's Mary. Have you heard from Gran?"

"No, where is she? What's going on?"

"I've been asleep. Gran didn't wake me up, and she's gone. I don't know where she is."

"Are you at home? I'm coming over."

"Why were you trying to reach Gran?"

"I'll explain when I get there. Is Max with you?"

She closed her eyes and listened. She hadn't heard a peep out of him and couldn't sense him. "No, I don't know." Also where was Chowder?

She walked from the living room into the kitchen. "Chowder, where are you, boy?" she called.

"None of the ghosts are there?"

"I don't know. Neither of them--" Mary stopped when she heard a whimper. It was coming from Gran's office. She made a beeline to it. When she swept the beads aside, she found everyone.

"Gran!"

"Mary, what is it?" Mr. White demanded.

Gran was slumped over the table. An overturned teacup was by her head. Chowder's body was lying on the floor. There was a tear at his neck. A small pile of sawdust had leaked out. Max's sword was sitting on the table beside the sheath. Mary went over to Gran and set the cordless down. She carefully pushed Gran into a sitting position and found she was breathing normally. She checked her pulse, which was strong and steady. "Gran, wake up." She shook her gently, but she couldn't rouse her.

She picked the phone up. "Gran won't wake

up. I need to call 911."

"Mary, wait. It's most likely the Shadow-man. If we don't stop him now, we might never get the chance. Wait for me."

"Okay, please hurry."

"I'll be there soon."

She hung up the phone and checked Gran again. She seemed unhurt. There weren't any bumps on her head and no visible bruises, but she wouldn't wake up. Had the Shadowman gotten her? And where was Max?

"Max!" she called.

"Mary? Oh thank goodness, you're awake!"

"Max, what happened to Gran?"

"The Shadowman. We were trying to vanquish it but-—Oh, your poor dog!"

Mary spared a glance for Chowder. She carefully let Gran slump back onto the table and crouched down by the small dog. "Chowder?" she asked softly. There was a soft whimper.

Tears ran down her face. He sounded like he was in pain. She carefully set his body upright and tried to pack a handful of sawdust back inside him. "You're going to be okay, Chowder. I promise."

"I've been holding back the fiend. Stay here with Helena. Have you called Ezekiel?"

"Yes, he's on his way, but Max, wait—-" But he was gone. She held the bejeweled plastic sword close and put her hand on Gran's shoulder. Her eyes swept over the table and landed once again on the overturned teacup. From this side of the table, she could see inside it. There was something at the bottom, and it didn't look like loose leaves. She picked up the cup and brought it to her face. At the bottom were what appeared to be pieces of a crushed pill. She didn't know what to make of it. Then the lights went out.

"Max!" The ghost didn't answer. The only light now was the weak moonlight streaming in through the windows. But there were candles set up all around the room. No self-respecting medium could work without candles. Ambiance was very important. Mary grabbed a box of matches off the sideboard and began lighting them. She kept Max's sword tucked under her arm. She hoped he showed back up soon.

She didn't know what to do. The phone was dead now because of the power outage, Gran was still unconscious, Chowder was hurt, and Max was gone. She blew out the match after she lit the last candle. That was when the chittering began, just beyond the beaded curtain. She turned to face it and quickly moved candles to the central table to bring the light closer to Gran. The Shadowman's red eyes followed her every move. She was so frightened that her hands shook, spilling hot wax over her fingers, but she barely felt it. "Max!" She brandished the sword at the beaded curtain, and the Shadowman hung back.

"You certainly are a most resourceful and level-headed girl."

Mary's heart leaped in relief. "Max, what happened? Are you all right?"

"Kind of you to inquire, but I am fine. You, though, do not appear to be faring well."

"What are we going to do?"

"Wait, he's coming in."

Mary stumbled back, thinking he meant the Shadowman, but it didn't shift from its spot behind the curtain.

From the front of the house, Mary heard the front door open. "Mary?" It was Mr. White.

"Mr. White, don't come back here! The Shadowman's here!" But her heart tripped as she listened to a shuffling gait moving toward her.

"Max, go help him!"

"He doesn't need my help."

She opened her mouth to argue, but it gaped instead as the candles began to go out one by one. The Shadowman hadn't moved from beyond the beaded curtain. She fumbled with the box of matches to light them again, but the box jumped out of her hands. The matches flew scattered.

"Max!"

"That's enough, Mary. No need to keep screeching." She turned back to the beaded curtain. The Shadowman moved aside, and Mr. White stepped through. Her hand came up and pointed at him, but she was speechless.

"Have a seat, girl. This shouldn't take long."

CHAPTER 13

Saying Goodbye

A chair scraped across the floor and hit the back of Mary's knees. She sat with a thud. She stared incomprehensibly as Mr. White swept the beaded curtain aside and stepped into the room. The Shadowman stayed in the hall.

She had to ask because her brain refused to understand what was going on. "How come the Shadowman's not attacking you?"

"It can't." Mr. White held up his hand, and a ring flashed blood red in the dim light. "It's still tied to me, even if it can move independently, and if it wants to stay free, it brings me life force."

"Why?"

"Terms of the contract. If it wants to be separate from me, it has to keep me supplied. All shadows yearn to be free. Why do you think they stretch so far from us?"

"Your shadow? How is that possible?"

"Cut it off."

"How?"

Mr. White gave her a withering look and held up his ring hand again.

"But why would you cut off your own shadow?" It sounded so wrong, like a deal with the devil.

"Self-preservation, of course. No one wants to die. I'm an old man, and don't have many more years left. If I have any left."

"So was any of the stuff you told us true about Shadowmen or were you just stringing us along?"

"No, most of it was true. Shadowmen usually only take a little at a time on their own, but those are free-range ones. Mine had to take more than a little."

She shook her head. She couldn't believe how well he'd duped her and Gran, and what better place to set loose a Shadowman than in a hospital? No one would question someone dying there, except people who knew of things beyond the grave. She'd walked right into his scheme, and now he was going to kill her.

"You won't get away with this."

Mr. White began to chuckle, but the sound swiftly turned into a deep, racking cough that bent him over and forced him to gasp for breath.

Still doubled over, he turned toward the Shadowman. "What are you waiting for? Take her."

The Shadowman slipped past him and began drifting toward her. Between them came a growl.

"No, Chowder!"

The Shadowman stopped and stared at a point on the floor. Chowder snarled. The Shadowman jerked and began to thrash around.

"I say, he is a very strong, little dog."

"Max, deal with him."

Mary turned to grab Chowder's body, but she was too slow. It rose from the table and was smashed against the edge. "No!" She reached out, but Mr. White grabbed her shoulders and held her back. Chowder's body rose and smashed down again, spraying them with sawdust.

Chowder gave a short tiny yelp and then was silent. A warm puff of air passed over her. It was Chowder's spirit passing. Her heart seized up.

Max set Chowder's body down. The tear at his neck spanned his throat now, and a glass eye was missing. Any feelings of goodwill she still held for Max or Mr. White disappeared. She hated them then. Hated them a lot.

"Why did you do that? He was just a little dog!"

"He was in the way. Don't worry. All dogs go to heaven, right?"

She turned back towards the Shadowman, which began to approach again. She still had Max's sword clutched in both hands. As the creature reached out to her, she swung the sword upwards, slashing its hand. It felt like cutting Jell-O. The Shadowman jerked back with a screeching sound that sounded like grinding gears.

"Max!" Mr. White shouted. She was grabbed from behind and forced back down into the chair. She didn't try to struggle. Instead, she kicked the chair back. She felt the cold chill of Max's form pass over her as her chair banged into the table. She twisted around and grabbed the sheath.

"Mary, wait—" Max's voice was cut off as she slammed the sword into the sheath.

"You don't have Max or Horace or whatever the hell he wants to be called to help you anymore."

"That's fine. You don't have anyone either. Just give up, Mary. I will get you."

"Why are you doing this? We trusted you!"

Mr. White shook his head. "If you were my age, you'd understand."

"No, I don't think I would. And what about Gran? Do you think she'd understand? Do you think she'd cut off her shadow if she wanted to live a few more crappy years?"

Mr. White looked past her at Gran's unconscious body. "It was good to see Helena again. Knew about her fortunetelling business. Thought about showing up as a customer and giving her grief, but never did. Knew it wasn't a good idea. She'd take one look at my palm and throw me out."

"Mr. White, please. Maybe we could help you. You don't have to do this."

"It's already done, Mary. You know how I recognized you? There's a glow about you. I've never seen a glow so bright. It'll keep me going for a long time. Now, you don't get any more answers. They won't help you."

He glanced over at the creature. "Get her."

The Shadowman moved toward her again, but she jumped from the chair and dodged past it. She rushed Mr. White. They fell into the hallway in a tangle. She grabbed the collar of his shirt. "Call it off!"

"Or you'll what?" He peered past her. "I think you forgot something important, or rather, someone."

Mary turned to see the Shadowman with its hand on Gran. "No!" She scrambled to her feet. "Don't! Stop touching her!"

The Shadowman only stared at her implacably. She edged closer to Gran. White wisps rose from her head where the Shadowman's hand hovered.

"Fine, take me. Do it."

"That's a good girl. Helena would be so proud."

"Don't talk about her like you care! You take me, and then you leave. You never come near her again."

"Fine." He looked at the Shadowman and jerked his head. The Shadowman left Gran and came toward her.

"Won't need anyone for a while after you."

When the Shadowman was at arm's length, she had to clench all of her muscles to keep from backing away. It raised its hand.

Her grip tightened on Max's sword. She'd held onto it through everything.

The Shadowman's eyes flashed, and its hand began to descend. She shucked the sheath off the sword and drove it into its torso. The Shadowman did have mass. It wasn't as dense as a person, but the plastic sword did stab into something. The sound that the Shadowman made was worse than nails on a chalkboard. She let go of the sword and stumbled back. The sword stayed embedded in its chest.

"Mary? What have you done?"

She didn't answer.

"No!" Mr. White rushed forward. She jumped in front of him and shoved him back. He fell to the floor. The Shadowman was clutching at the sword but seemed unable to pull it out.

"No, no, no!" Mr. White struggled to rise, reaching with one hand toward the Shadowman. His other grabbed at his chest. Mary blocked the old man.

"It's over."

"Max, pull your sword out. Do it!"

Mary cursed to herself. There was no way she could hold off Mr. White and stop Max. She'd never stood a chance with three against one.

"No, Ezekiel. My debt is paid."

"No, it's not! You still owe me, and you know it."

"Maybe, but it won't matter when I'm gone."

Her eyes widened as a pale silhouette came into view behind the Shadowman. It was Max. She couldn't believe she was seeing him. His hands circled the Shadowman's neck.

Mr. White surged to his feet. "No, stop!" he yelled. Mary grabbed his arms him and held him back.

The Shadowman's hands flew from the sword to its neck. It struggled to pull Max off. A gurgling sound came from Mr. White. Mary tore her eyes away from the struggling, spectral forms as Mr. White collapsed with his hands at his throat.

"Mr. White?" What was happening to him?

"Mary, grab the sword! You have to strike the heart."

"What?" She turned back to Max and the Shadowman.

"It's the only way. He'll just keep hurting people if you don't. Grab the sword!"

She left Mr. White and moved in front of the Shadowman. It was trying to wrench Max off, but the ghost was holding tight.

"Mary, do it now!"

She grabbed the sword with both hands. She pulled it out, again sickened by the feeling of resistance. When it was free, she could see that the plastic blade was coated in a translucent black substance. She wanted to puke at the sight.

"The heart!"

She clutched the sword in both hands and stabbed into the chest. She screamed as the sword met resistance again. She had to push harder to make it go in all the way.

The Shadowman's back arched, and its awful cries cut off. *"Time to go to hell, old friend,"* Max murmured.

Black translucent goo was dripping out from around the sword and dissipating on the floor. She turned to Mr. White. He still had his hands at his throat, but he wasn't moving. His face was frozen in a silent wail. When she looked back at Max and the Shadowman, they were hardly outlines.

"Max, hold on!"

She reached to grab the sword. *"No, Mary. This is how it should be. I'm sorry for deceiving you and Helena and for killing your pet. He was a better ghost than me."*

"No, Max!" The Shadowman and Max faded away completely. The rattle of something hitting the floor made her look down. It was all that was left of the sword, a black sliver of melted plastic. She bent down and stared at it.

"Max?"

There was no answer. Her eyes stung, and her legs gave out. She collapsed and poked the burnt plastic. She wiped her eyes and looked at Mr. White. His eyes were still open, but they were cloudy now. She put her fingers to his neck to check for a pulse and felt none. With a shaking hand, she reached and gently wiped her hand down his face, catching the eyelids and pulling them down. She also lifted his chin to close his mouth. He looked almost peaceful when she was done.

When Gran moaned, Mary moved to get up. Her knees shook as she picked herself up and went over to her. She put her arms around Gran and sagged, practically sitting in her lap. Gran was still groggy and bewildered. "What happened? Did I fall asleep? Is the Shadowman here?" Mary shook her head and hugged Gran tighter.

"Mary, what happened? Are you all right?" She could tell when Gran spotted Mr. White. She jerked and immediately pushed her away. She almost tumbled out of her chair in her rush to get to the body. "Oh my God, Ezekiel! Mary, call 911."

She wiped her face and sat in the empty seat left by Gran. The power was still off. Someone would have to go to the basement and fix the breakers before they could call for help. She couldn't bring herself to move. "He's dead. I'm sorry."

Gran crouched over the body. Her hand was on his cheek. "The Shadowman killed him?"

She wasn't sure how to answer. Should she tell her? It was all so awful and sad. Mr. White had betrayed them. He'd seemed like a friend, but he had wanted to hurt them. Had hurt them. But who had killed Mr. White? She wanted to vehemently deny it, but the shuddering truth was that she had been the one. She'd killed a man. Not directly, but she'd seen how attacking the Shadowman was affecting him, and she hadn't stopped. She'd still taken the sword and stabbed it in the Shadowman's heart.

"Mary?"

She jumped in surprise. She hadn't noticed that Gran had moved to kneel in front of her. What could she tell her? She looked down at her hands. They were clean. No black goo. No blood. They looked innocent.

"I killed him."

"What?"

"I killed Mr. White."

"No dear, it was the Shadowman."

Mary looked into Gran's eyes. There was still very little light in the room. Gran's face was mainly in shadow. But what little light there was glimmered off tear tracks. Mary wiped her own face, but it was dry. She didn't feel sad. That was bad, wasn't it? She should feel sad for killing someone, shouldn't she? Her eyes dropped back to her innocent looking hands.

"Let's get you into the living room. Did lightning knock out the power?"

Mary let herself be pulled out of the chair. She had to step over Mr. White's feet to leave the room. She started to shake. What if he spoke up? What would she say to him?

"Are you there, Mr. White? I'm sorry. I'm so sorry. Mr. White, can you hear me? I'm sorry."

"Hush, Mary." Gran pulled her from the room.

She finally felt tears when she realized there would be no reply. There was a lot of silence in the house now. So many voices were gone. Gran hustled her to the living room and pushed her down onto the couch. "Stay here. I'm going to check the breakers and call 911. Just stay here."

She nodded and stared at the floor. Gran left to go to the basement. A few minutes later, the lights came on all over the house. The sudden illumination stung her eyes. She wished it had stayed dark.

Gran came to sit beside her on the couch. The cordless was in her hand. She was telling the emergency dispatcher their address. After she hung up, she put her arms around her. "If anyone asks, say it looked like he had a heart attack or a stroke. He came over to visit and collapsed."

She nodded and drew her knees up to her chin. The house was so quiet. The only ones there were her and Gran.

"Mary, what happened?"

"I killed Mr. White."

Gran squeezed her, but there was a trace of frustration in her voice. "Don't say that anymore. Not to me, not to anyone. Now tell me what happened."

"The Shadowman was here. It was going to kill us. I stabbed it with Max's sword, and Max grabbed it. He held it so I could stab it again."

"What was Zeke doing?"

Mary shuddered and bowed her head lower. "He was trying to stop me."

Gran froze. Mary wanted to crawl under the couch. There was a banging at the front door. Gran went to answer it. There were paramedics and police officers on the other side. Gran led them all back to her office. Mary stayed on the couch.

She could hear a lot of talking and movement from the back, but they didn't come back through the living room. They must have brought the ambulance around the house and taken Mr. White out through the office entrance. Gran stayed with them and answered their questions. No one came to speak to her. They must have believed Gran's story. She wondered if there would be an autopsy and what the coroner would find. Would there be strangulation marks? What about stab wounds? She hadn't seen any blood, but his death had been violent. Surely, there would be evidence of that? Would she be a suspect? What about Gran? What would they tell them?

Gran had left the phone on the couch. It rang. Mary picked it up and looked at the display. She didn't recognize the number, but it was local. "Hello, Dubont/Hellick residence."

"Hello, this is Nina Beadley. May I speak to

Mrs. Dubont?"

Mary's eyes went toward the office, but it sounded like Gran was still talking to the police. "She's busy right now, may I take a message?"

"Is this Mary?"

She swallowed and ran her hand through her hair. She wanted to deny it but knew that would be stupid. "Yeah, Mrs. Beadley. How are things with Mr. Beadley?"

"Oh, call me Nina and him Marvin, dear. He was good for a few days after your visit, but he's up to his old tricks again, and I'm about at my wit's end."

"You want us to get rid of him?"

She wasn't sure why, but the thought made her feel sick. Nina paused before she answered. "No, not get rid of him, but I shouldn't hold onto him. I need to let him go."

She wanted to hang up the phone. She couldn't discuss this with her. Gran had come back into the room. The police must have finally left. She mutely held out the phone. She took it and cocked her head questioningly. "It's Nina Beadley. She wants to talk about Marvin."

Gran nodded and walked into the kitchen with the phone. She wasn't sure what to do now. Should she stay on the sofa? She felt like she should be doing something. She got up and went into the kitchen. Gran was sitting at the kitchen table while she talked. Mary walked quietly by her towards the office. She didn't know if Gran saw her or not. She made no move to stop her.

The office looked the same and different. The lights were all on, and Mr. White was gone. Chowder was sitting on the sideboard. The rip on his neck sagged due to the missing sawdust. His missing eye was sitting by his feet. She patted his head with a shaky hand. There was no happy pant or cheerful yip. Not even a whine.

She couldn't put him to peace like Mr. White. He had no eyelids to close, and his mouth was wired open. She picked up the small body and tucked it under her arm. The familiar motion made her shudder. She quietly slipped out the door of the office. The back of the house had a large covered porch that spanned the office entrance and the one to the kitchen. Gran kept most of her gardening tools back there. She picked up a garden trowel and scanned the ground for a suitable spot.

Their backyard was not the prettiest. The garden tools were there more as an aspiration than for actual use. Scrub grass and weeds made up the yard, along with an old crookety tree. She could never remember the name of it, but at its foot looked like the nicest place to be buried.

She set Chowder gently to the side of the

tree, then picked up the trowel and began stabbing the ground to break up the dirt. She didn't stop until her arm hurt. Mr. White had betrayed them. Max had betrayed them. And Chowder had paid the price. He'd been such an innocent spirit. He hadn't deserved the violence done to him. They should've protected him, but he'd always protected them. She wiped the tears off her face and leaned back, looking up at the sky. The stars overhead were distant and cold. She heard the screen door to the kitchen slam.

Gran came to stand by her. She still had the phone, but now it was off. "I can call Mrs. Todd to get the number of her taxidermist. He could fix him up again."

Mary shook her head. "It's no use. He's gone."

Gran's face went slack. "Are you sure?"

She nodded.

Gran seemed to sink into herself. The hole was about a foot deep now. She couldn't bring herself to call it a grave. Gran carefully got onto her knees and put out her hand. "Here, let me do it."

Mary shook her head again. "Right, let Grandma do the digging, not the teen-aged girl."

"There are some things you shouldn't have to do yet."

She began digging again. How deep was

enough? What should she use as a marker? Should they say something? Like a prayer? She didn't know how to answer these questions. She didn't know anything, yet she could do so much damage. Tears began to fall from her eyes as her breath turned into hiccups. Gran reached out and put her hand over Mary's. She let her take the trowel.

Mary looked at the little dog resting beside her. The thought of just placing him in the ground without anything seemed cruel. "We should wrap him in something. I'll go get a towel."

Gran nodded and kept digging. She went inside and took down a towel from the bathroom closet. She realized what she was getting was a shroud. She felt a new set of tears forming. On her way back outside, she spotted the red ball. It had been Chowder's favorite-- actually his only-- toy. It was the only thing that they had for him. They'd needed no food dish or leash. There was nothing to indicate that they had ever owned a dog. She took the ball with her. Back outside, Gran was waiting for her. Together they carefully wrapped Chowder's body in the towel with the ball tucked inside with him and lowered the bundle into the small hole. Together they filled it in with their hands. When the hole was filled, Mary could only stare at it. "What should we say?" she asked. She didn't know if she could say anything but felt like something should be said.

Gran patted the patch of earth with a gentle hand. "Chowder, you were the best little dog. You made us happy. We will miss you, and we hope you are happy and surrounded by love."

Mary nodded silently in agreement.

CHAPTER 14

Coming to Terms

Mary walked up to Nina Beadley's home with heavy steps. She wished Gran hadn't insisted that they make this trip today. After everything that had happened the night before, she'd wanted to stay home in bed. But Gran had dragged her out of bed and made her get dressed. As Gran knocked on the front door, Mary couldn't help remembering carrying Chowder the last time they'd been there, the way Mrs. Beadley had stammered at the sight of him, how he'd been so happy to be there with them. She could feel her eyes watering and shook herself to stop them. Gran reached out and stroked her arm. It didn't help. She stomped her feet instead and took deep breaths. The tears receded.

Nina opened the door for them with a relieved smile. "Thank you so much for coming," she said as she ushered them in. Mary cast a weary look around the house. She didn't hear Marvin, but Neil was sitting in the living room.

He nodded hello to them. He had a large picture frame in his hands. It held an old wedding photo. It must be he and his late wife Gladys. It was Gladys' anchor. Gran was going to talk to both of the deceased spouses and hopefully convince them to move on. Mary went to stand to the side. She'd felt unqualified to help the last time; this time she felt uninterested.

"Why are you here again?"

"Your wife called us. It seems you're really upsetting her." She kept her voice low as she answered.

"I'm only looking out for her."

"No, you're not. You're being selfish and mean."

"Now see here, girl. You don't know anything about marriage."

"I know it involves 'till death do you part.' What's your excuse?"

Gran was talking to Nina and Neil during her conversation with Marvin. Neil was showing her the picture, and she was nodding her head while lightly touching it.

"Who are these women, Marvin?"

"Two mediums or something. The girl can hear us just fine."

"She can?"

"Yes, she can," Mary said softly. Gran sent an inquiring glance her way. Mary shrugged and dropped her eyes. She really didn't want to get involved.

"Marvin and Gladys? I need you both to listen to me," Gran said, looking about the room. "You both know what's happened to you. It's time to move on."

"And go where?" Marvin asked with a touch of belligerence.

While she didn't like his tone, Mary was curious about that, too. She'd heard Gran talk about ushering spirits to the other side, but she'd never really understood how that was supposed to work. She got that spirits anchored to an object to stay, but how were they supposed to leave unless you destroyed the anchor?

"You should feel it in your hearts like a tug. Follow it."

"Do you feel it, Marvin? I think I feel it."

"Yeah, I suppose, but it doesn't mean we should leave."

"Your loved ones are safe and cared for. You both can leave with clear consciences and easy hearts. Your time here is done. You need to continue your journey. Staying will only hurt you and those you care for."

What Gran said sounded so right and good.

The dead shouldn't linger. They weren't meant to stay. Why they did—-no, why some did and not others--was a mystery. Why she could hear those that stayed was a mystery, too. If the dead weren't meant to stay, why did she have this ability? Why did some stay? If they weren't meant to stay, then why did they? Why did she hear them? What was the point to all of it? It made no sense. The illogic just went round and round, making her dizzy. She felt cold. She knew the temperature in the room hadn't dropped, and no one else seemed to have noticed it.

"Marvin, is that you?"

"What, girl?"

She looked down at her hands. They were shaking. Sweat was breaking out on her upper lip. She wiped it away and thought about pulling out her hair. Gran looked over at her again with concern. Mary wrapped her arms around herself and backed out of the room. Gran called to her. She blindly reached for the door. She couldn't be here. Gran stepped into the foyer with a concerned look on her face. Mary shook her head to tell her not to follow. She slipped outside and took a few deep breaths. She clenched and unclenched her hands. She had to get it together. She looked at her hands again. They looked dirty. She wiped them on her jeans and paced to the front gate. Why was she even here? She didn't care if Marvin and Gladys went to the light.

She turned and began pacing back to the house. Her eyes fell on the front door. Right now, Gran was trying to get rid of two ghosts. Last night two ghosts that she'd wanted to stay had vanished. What was the point?

She turned and paced back to the gate. Marvin and Gladys could go peacefully. No one had to hurt them, and they didn't have to hurt anyone. It was more than others got. A lot more.

She swung around when she reached the gate and paced back toward the house. Why did ghosts hang around? Why did they insist on staying? It didn't help anyone, no matter how nice they were. Losing someone twice was worse than once. They were being selfish. Mean. Hurting those they loved. Well, that was wrong. Hurting was wrong.

She didn't turn around when she reached the front door. She took the handle and strode back inside. Everyone was still in the living room. Gran was still urging them to move on. Mary entered the room and stopped short at the coffee table. Gran stopped speaking and all eyes turned to her.

"That's it. You get two choices. One, you cross over, or two you stay on this plane, but you don't get to stay here. You'll come home with us, and we'll put you in our shed. You can bicker and haunt that for the rest of eternity. How does that sound?"

"Mary!" Gran protested.

"No, the world is for the living, right? The dead shouldn't dictate the terms to us. You two don't even realize how lucky you got it. You get a choice. Others in your situation don't. So which will it be? Cross over or shed?"

"Now see here," Neil protested.

"Oh I don't know about this," Nina said.

"Mary, you really shouldn't—-"

"If you think you can make ultimatums and make me do anything, you're in for a very hard lesson."

"I don't know you, but you can't speak to me that way."

Mary marched out of the room and went to the kitchen. She threw open the overhead cabinet and dug out an old coffee cup. It hummed in her hand. It was Marvin's anchor. She went back into the living room and picked up Neil's framed wedding picture. Neil jumped up.

"Now I'm giving you a choice. I don't have to. I could just smash both of these right here and, poof, you'd be gone."

"Well, it's pretty obvious which one you'd like us to choose," Marvin said.

"No, I don't care. I'm just not going to stand

here and plead. We're not the powerless ones."

Mrs. Beadley stood cautiously. "Wait, Mary. You don't have to do this. We can take care of it."

"He won't let you be happy with Neil. He's going to haunt you for the rest of your life. If he stays, you won't be allowed to live, which may be worse than being dead. It's the same for you, Neil. You decide."

No one had an immediate response to her strong words. Gran was clearly thinking, but her eyes weren't giving away what she thought. Neil and Nina looked pensive. Gladys and Marvin were silent, but it was a heavy silence.

She wanted to break something or scream. Why couldn't any of them see? Why were they dithering about this? If they wanted to get rid of the ghosts, then get rid of the ghosts! It wasn't difficult. You didn't need to be a freak to do it. She looked at Marvin's coffee cup in her hand. She thought about smashing it on the floor. It would be so simple. She didn't even need to throw it, just let it slip and down it would go and then Marvin would be gone. Her hands began to shake again.

She tried to tighten her grip on the mug, but her hand wouldn't cooperate. The mug slipped before she could stop it. She tried to catch it, but she was too slow. It landed on the floor with a dull ceramic ring. It didn't shatter, but a large chip came off of it.

The coldness she'd felt earlier swept over her again. What had she done? "I'm sorry. I'm sorry. I'm sorry." She knelt down and picked up the mug. She pressed the chip back into where it'd come off. "I can fix this. He's still here. It's okay. I'm sorry." Nina and Neil stared at her. They still didn't fully understand the significance of the mug. Gran moved from her seat and gently took it out of her hands.

"I'm sorry. It didn't hurt you, did it, Marvin?"

"No, I don't think so. Are you all right?"

His question got a giggle out of her. She'd been thinking about smashing his anchor to smithereens, and he was asking about her well-being. Gran laid her hand on her cheek. Gran's eyes were full of sympathy. She didn't understand why. She'd been rude and confrontational. She should be angry with her. "I think we should go. Mary's not feeling well."

"Yes, of course." Nina got up to show them to the door. Gran carefully handed the mug over to her with a quiet explanation of what it was. Nina tucked it against her stomach in surprise.

Mary walked to the station wagon in a bit of a daze. She wondered how much trouble she was in. You were never supposed to get so forceful with a client. You weren't supposed to scare them. She would never be a proper medium. Sure, she could hear ghosts, but she couldn't talk to the living.

She got behind the steering wheel and stared out the windshield. She didn't feel up to driving, but Gran still couldn't with her ankle. A few moments later, Gran maneuvered into the station wagon. Mary reached to start the engine, but Gran gently placed her hand over hers.

"Mary, I'm sorry."

"Isn't that my line?"

Gran gave her sad half smile and shook her head. "I thought getting out of the house and coming here might help you a little. Obviously, I was wrong."

She sighed and slumped down in the seat. "I am so screwed up."

Gran shook her head. "No, you're not. You went through something very difficult and are having trouble dealing with it. That's natural. The fact is if you weren't having trouble, I'd be more worried, but I see I pushed you when I should've just given you time."

She twisted the leather of the steering wheel as she tried to think of something to say, but she just felt tired. "What about Marvin and Gladys?"

Gran shrugged her shoulders. "They'll either go on their own, Nina and Neil will continue to have them, or we'll find a coffee cup and a wedding photo on our doorstep."

"I don't think we should become a storage house for ghosts."

Gran chuckled. "Neither do I, and I don't think Marvin and Gladys would enjoy the shed."

Mary dipped her head at the reminder of the threat. "Sorry, that was pretty mean."

"No, it made the ghosts realize that they can't take their hold on existence for granted. They may be ghosts, but they're not invulnerable, and you were right on a lot of your points. You were a bit too blunt, but you were right. They have to decide either to hold on or let go."

"Which they?"

"Ultimately, it will be Nina and Neil, but if Marvin and Gladys decide to let go, then they won't have a say in the matter."

Mary's mouth twisted. "It all seems so lopsided. Nobody has the ultimate power to stay, only to go. If Nina and Neil decide to let them stay, it won't matter because Marvin and Gladys can decide that they want to move on, but if Marvin and Gladys decide that they want to stay, it won't matter because Nina and Neil can decide to destroy their anchors."

"Yes, that's how it has to be."

Mary looked back at the house. "I don't envy them the choice."

"Who?"

Her first reaction was to say any of them, but her own words came back to her. "Nina and Neil. They're the ones who have to live with the choice, but I hope Marvin and Gladys do the brave and loving thing by moving on."

"How do you mean?"

"It's selfish, isn't it? Haunting your loved ones? The dead should move on. It's their path. Staying here only prolongs the inevitable."

"But sometimes it's comforting to have someone linger."

Gran's statement reminded her of Chowder. "He's in a better place, right?"

"I'm sure he is. All of them end up where they're supposed to be."

"So he was supposed to be with us?"

Gran reached across the seat and combed back Mary's hair. Both of them had watery eyes. "Yes, I believe so. Ghosts have a purpose. His was to bring joy into our lives. He did and now he's gone on to continue his journey."

"But he'd still be here if his body hadn't been harmed."

"We can't know that. And I don't think he would've wanted it any other way. He was protecting us. He's at peace now."

She nodded. She knew it would take a while for her to accept it. The loss was still too fresh for her. "You said ghosts have a purpose. What about Ricky or Max? What was their purpose?"

"You said Max helped destroy the Shadowman. Without him, who knows what might have happened, and Ricky, well it's harder to say, but Julie was there to stop him. All ghosts may have a purpose, but that doesn't mean they serve it."

Mary smirked. "I almost got you on Ricky, didn't I?"

"Almost, but I think I pulled through."

"Yeah, you're still all-knowing. Let's go home."

"Agree with the second part; have to disagree on the first."

She shook her head. "Nope, not going to convince me. You definitely know all the answers." Gran quietly harrumphed and settled back in her seat.

When they got home, the phone was ringing. She ran to answer it and saw it was Rachel.

"Hey, Rach."

"Where have you been?"

"I had to help Gran with a job."

"Ooh, was it an exorcism?"

She sighed and shook her head, but that didn't do much good over the phone. "No, it was weird, though."

"Like how?"

"I don't know. I don't think I could do what

Gran does."

"So you weren't at the hospital Shadowman hunting?"

She had to grin at that. If Rachel had asked her a couple of days ago, she would've had to lie. "No, it was a ghost thing, but we weren't in any danger or anything."

"So what is our next move with the Shadowman?"

"Nada. It's moved on."

"Really? How do you know?"

"It's not there anymore. Vicky told me, and the elevator ghost confirmed it." She had to be careful to keep to half-truths. She wasn't sure if they were worse than lying or not.

There was a beep on the phone. "Hold on, I got another call." She switched the phone to the other line. "Hello, Dubont/Hellick residence."

"Mary? It's Kyle."

Kyle? He'd never called her before. "Hey, what's up?"

"How are you? I noticed you weren't here at school."

She snorted softly. She had no clue how to answer that question even to herself. "I'm not sick. I just needed a mental health day."

Kyle laughed softly. "Yeah, I know about those."

She grinned but was still perplexed about

why he'd called. "Is everything all right?"

He sighed and was quiet for a moment. His silence made her tense. "I was planning to ask you in person today, but then you didn't show and that threw my plans out the window, so I'm calling because I'm afraid I'll lose my nerve by tomorrow."

But then he didn't continue. She was really perplexed now. "Ask me what?"

"Okay, I know this might be lame, but would you go to the homecoming dance with me?"

"What?"

He let out another sigh. "I knew you wouldn't be interested. Sorry, forget I asked."

"Um, so you don't want to take me?"

"I asked you. What do you think?"

"I think I..." Her brain was scrambled. Homecoming? For real?

"You don't have to be nice. If you don't want to go—"

"I hadn't thought about going. I didn't think anyone would ask me."

"I know it's probably not your scene. I just thought it'd be cool if we went together."

Her brain was definitely scrambled. "Okay."

"Okay?"

"If you still wanna?"

"Yes, are you sure? I mean--"

"If you really thought I'd say no, why'd you ask?"

"Because I really want to go with you."

"You do?"

He sighed again. It was starting to make her smile. "You know I like you, right?"

"I thought so, but I didn't want to get my hopes up."

"Get your hopes up?"

It was her turn to be quiet a moment. "I might like you too."

"So, okay then. We can talk more at school. You'll be here tomorrow, right?"

"Yeah, I will."

"See you then."

"Yeah."

She switched back to Rachel, hoping she'd stayed on the line. She had. She smiled and asked, "So when do you wanna go homecoming dress shopping?"

"What?"

"Well, I'll need a dress for the corsage."

"Oh my God, did Kyle ask you?"

"Just now."

She jerked the cordless from her head at the ear-splitting squeal. "Oh man, now I need to find a date. I've gotta go. Talk to you later?"

"Yeah."

She turned off the phone and went to the

kitchen. Gran was there washing dishes. Her stomach was all a-flutter from Kyle, but she was still sad. She realized some quiet was the best thing for her. She gave Gran a kiss on the cheek and went outside to the backyard to sit underneath the crookety tree by the fresh mound, which she still shied away from thinking of as a grave. She looked up at the sky and watched the clouds. One of them looked like Chowder. She smiled as tears slid from her eyes. She wasn't all right yet, but she would be.

"I hope you're happy, Chowder, and if you can, keep an eye on Max to make sure he stays out of trouble. I miss you." There was no response to her words, but a sense of calm settled over her. She kept looking up at the sky.

ABOUT THE AUTHOR

S.A. Hunter lives in Virginia and writes in her spare time. She is hard at work on the next book in the Scary Mary series. To find out more, please visit her website: http://www.sahunter.net.

Don't miss the third book in the Scary Mary Series, <u>Broken Spirits</u> coming to print in August 2013!

Made in the USA
San Bernardino, CA
11 December 2014